FROST

WINTER'S LONELY GUARDIAN

EE RAWLS

FROST, Winter's Lonely Guardian.
Copyright © by author E.E. Rawls 2022
All rights reserved

Cover art by Leejun35

This is a work of fiction. Names, characters, businesses, places, events, locales, and incidents are either the products of the author's imagination or used in a fictitious manner. Any resemblance to actual persons, living or dead, or actual events is purely coincidental.

Associated logos and art are trademarks of author E.E. Rawls. All related characters and elements are trademarks of E.E. Rawls.

This book or any portion thereof may not be reproduced or used in any manner whatsoever without the express written permission of the publisher except for the use of brief quotations in a book review or book promotion.

ISBN: 979-8-9852392-1-8 paperback
ISBN: 979-8-9852392-2-5 hardback

www.eerawls.com

Printed in the U.S.A.
First edition, November 2022

Titles by E.E. Rawls

Earthaverse:

~

Draev Guardians Series

Strayborn (1)

Storm & Choice (0.5)

Dragons & Ravens (1.5)

Strayblood (2)

Alteredverse:

~

Frost

Portal to Eartha

Beast of the Night

Madness Solver in Wonderland

Coming Soon:

Straypath (3)

Plus several "secret projects" ;)

Find out when the next books are releasing, and get exclusive content, by following my newsletter at:
eerawls.com

Jack Frost, Jack Frost,
Came in the night;
Left the meadows that he crossed
All gleaming white.
Painted with his silver brush
Every window-pane.
Kissed the leaves and made them blush,
Blush and blush again.

—Poem "Jacky Frost"
by Laura E. Richards

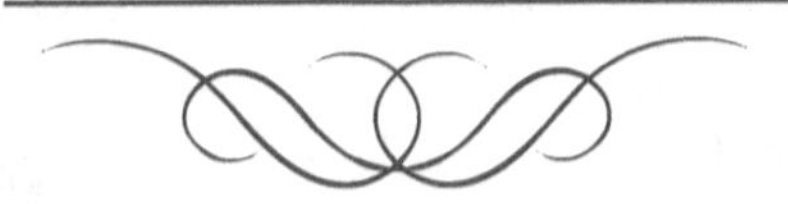

Year 1885

ENDRE TIPPED BACK THE BRIM of his hat to better see the magnificent steamship waiting at the docks before them, the tall stacks puffing out billows of gray into the pale blue sky. He gripped the handle of his leather suitcase in anticipation.

"Endre, don't dawdle," his mother called and motioned with a hurried hand for him to join them, as they stood waiting in line to board the ship.

Ada began tugging on his free hand relentlessly. His little sister was excited for their first ever trip beyond the borders of England. "Cannot be late, cannot be late!" she chorused, pulling him into the line of boarding passengers. Mother smiled and patted Ada's flowery bonnet when they reached her side.

"Sometimes I think your sister is the elder one," she mused. "She listens more than you do."

Endre rolled his eyes and shifted the heavy suitcase, eager for the line to move faster, itching to get onboard and explore.

Father tapped his shoulder. "Don't worry, we'll have lunch as soon as we get our luggage to our room," he said, assuming that Endre must be fidgeting due to hunger. "Then you can both have some fun and explore the ship's deck," he added.

Endre bobbed his head. He focused his attention on a seagull that had caught an updraft, gliding gracefully overhead before dipping low to the ocean's gray waves where its yellow bill snatched something from the waters.

The line moved on up the great boarding ramp. Ada gripped the rope railing, making it swing back and forth until Father made her stop. With a pout of boredom, she began poking at Endre's suitcase and demanding to know everything he had packed inside it.

Endre huffed. He tried to recite the list of items to entertain her. "Spare shoes, a sweater, the little dog Uncle carved me..."

"You brought the dog?" Ada laughed.

"What's wrong with that?" He pouted. "Even Mr. Woof wanted a vacation away from stuffy old England."

She continued laughing uproariously, and Mother had to shush them both, casting apologetic glances to the elderly couples standing near them, who frowned disdainfully.

By the time they got onboard the steamship and found their small room, Endre collapsed in hunger and mental exhaustion upon one of the tiny, narrow beds. Mother chuckled as she put their suitcases against the wall.

The blast of a horn sounded when the steamship began its departure, and Endre hurried outside to the deck rails with

Ada in tow. They waved to the people standing on the docks, Endre waving his hat, and he watched as the people shrank to the size of ants and the coastal English buildings became a fuzzy smudge, blending into the rest of the landscape on either side of the wide waterway.

After a couple hours, the land faded away from sight as the ship entered the open waters of St. George's Channel. The seagulls eventually took their leave of the rails, unwilling to make the full journey with them across to Ireland.

Endre and his family soon made their way to the dining hall, a lavish space of shiny surfaces and rich furnishings. The food wasn't quite to their standards from back home, though, which disappointed him. The pasties all had too soggy bottoms.

Endre chose the vegetable soup and bread instead, and shoveled it into his mouth. Ada whined that the veg hadn't been cooked tenderly enough, much to Mother's exasperation.

"No more complaining, Ada. Eat your food. There will be plenty of tender vegetables once we reach your uncle in Ireland."

Endre spent the rest of his time out on deck, keeping a lookout for dolphins or for any sea creatures from folklore that might be lurking nearby. If a kraken's tentacle touched the ship's hull, he would sound the alarm and go into battle!

He eyed the gray-blue waters intensely. He hadn't been outside long when he noticed the horizon was quickly filling up with clouds. The sun became obscured, and the wind forced him to take off his hat and hold it close.

Ada, who had tagged along with him, soon became bored and went back below decks to find Mother.

That evening, the steamship rocked along the growing waves while dinner was served to the passengers.

Endre nibbled at a bread roll but couldn't stomach

anything more with the rocking motion below their feet.

"Mummy, make the ship stop moving," Ada whined. Mother rubbed her back soothingly.

The adults were unsettled; he caught the worried looks they tried to hide around the dining hall as the rocking motion continued.

Endre moved to the thick door that let outside onto the deck and peered through the glass window there. Lightning forked through the sky and rain pelted the deck's sleek surface. He could also make out the dark shape of land, not far away.

They must have finished crossing the open waters to Ireland and were now hugging the coastline towards their destined port.

"Endre, come away from there," Mother chastised him. "It's not safe outdoors in this storm."

"I was only looking. I wasn't going outside," he protested. "We've reached Ireland! If only I could see it without all the fog..."

Mother grabbed his hand, pulling him back. "You will, once the ship docks. But right now, it's past your bedtime, and we won't reach the port for another few hours."

He grumbled and complained. It would have been much more fun to watch the storm, but she dragged him away.

Inside their cramped bedroom, Endre was too excited for sleep, and he tossed and turned in the tiny, thin bed. Ada groaned beside him, rubbing her tummy.

"Why does my tummy feel sick?" she whined.

He turned his head to face her. The answer seemed obvious to him, so he decided to share his knowledge to prove how smart he was, by saying, "You've got sea sickness."

Ada's face scrunched up across the pillow. "Got what?"

"Sea sickness," he repeated. "It's what happens to people who aren't used to ships. The storm's making it worse, too, rocking the ship all about. The only cure is to stand outside and focus your eyes on any nearby land, or on the horizon." He smiled, proud of himself for knowing so much. Reading books about ship voyages had paid off!

Ada's lips pursed in thought. She groaned again and turned to face the other way.

Endre yawned and tried to fall asleep. His imagination ran wild with thoughts of giant sea creatures bumping the ship back and forth with their fins and getting ready to bite a massive hole through the hull.

After another restless length of time, he gave up trying to sleep and instead leaned over to poke Ada. But his sister didn't stir. In fact, she felt more like a lumpy pillow than flesh.

He poked again. Then he pulled back the sheet and found that it was, in fact, a pillow.

"Ada?" he called as quietly as he could. But she wasn't anywhere in their shared bed. He sat up and blinked about the room, but the candlelight from the nearby lamp didn't show her in their parents' bed either.

Curious what his sister could be up to, he put on his shoes and coat and slipped out their room and into the corridor. Boards creaked and groaned against the pressure of the rocking waves as he shuffled along the polished floor and peered into any open doors. The dining hall was clear, the commons room clear, the lavatories clear—as far as he was able to tell without being indecent and entering past the door.

Lastly, he trotted up the stairs and checked the door to the upper deck. The storm grumbled outside the door's window, and there hanging onto the ship railing was a huge bird.

What would a bird be doing there, in this weather? Loony creature!

No, it wasn't a bird, he realized with a start—it was a person. The flapping feathers was a nightgown whipped by the wind.

"Ada!" He yanked open the door and ran outside to her, the rain pelting him like a torrent of pebbles. The ship lurched, and he slipped on the slick deck, catching himself on the railing before he could fall. He looked, but Ada was no longer there.

Panic pounded inside his chest, matching the rumbling thunder overhead.

"Adaaa!" he called again, shifting to scan the ocean below.

An object bobbed in the swelling waves close to the ship: a pink nightgown—Ada.

Endre grabbed the nearest floatation device: a cork vest, tied to the wall, and without thinking he jumped over the rail.

He hit the water hard, receiving a cold and painful shock to his system.

He paddled his arms and sucked in air, fighting off the shock, and tried to search for Ada. She was barely afloat, but he had landed near enough to her that he reached her in a few strokes and wrapped the cork vest around her arms.

She was coughing up water, shaking and unable to speak. He realized, then, that he had no way of getting them both back onboard the ship. So, he did the next best thing and screamed for help, and held Ada close.

"Oi!"

He lifted his head at the replying shout and saw a rope land in the water, tossed by one of the sailors. The waves were beginning to pull them away from the ship, and Endre used every bit of his strength to kick and paddle and reach the rope. When he finally grasped its slick fibers, he looped the rope around Ada's body and told her to hold on tight, though he wasn't sure if she could hear him above the storm's roar.

He held onto the rope as several sailors gathered to pull them up. The waves rolled and he could feel the current tugging him, pulling on him like the hands of evil water fae determined to drown him.

The sailors were having trouble reigning in the limp rope; the lurch of the ship was such that it threatened to snap the fibers if they were not careful. Beside him, Ada was turning blue, and he could barely feel her chest breathing.

If she didn't get out of the frigid waters soon, she would die. There was no time to fight the pull of the current—he had to lessen the weight on the rope, or else risk both of them dying.

"Ada," he said, and gasped for air. "I love you."

He let go of the rope.

Endre could just make out the sight of Ada being pulled closer to the ship's side before nothing but waves filled his vision. He rose and fell, carried by the swells, and the cold weight of his clothes dragged him under. He fought to reach air, again and again, until the muscles in his arms and legs cramped and gave out. He urged them to move, but the cold was like a vise, and he could feel himself sinking further and further.

I'm going to die.

He ceased to struggle and let his body sink, limp beneath the raging storm above.

He dearly hoped it would not be painful.

Something glinted in the darkness of the ocean. A flick of a fish tail.

And there came a vague sense of being carried…

When his hands later felt rocks beneath him, he coughed up saltwater and opened his eyes. Everything was still dark. Using his elbows, he crawled forward, up a slope of rocks that he could feel, and pulled himself the rest of the way out of the waves, the crashing clamor of them filling his ears from behind.

He crawled onward, feeling a trickle of a freshwater stream around him amidst the rocks, and he rested against a curved wall of some sort.

Stars glowed and flickered overhead with a strange teal light. After a while of catching his breath, and regaining his senses, Endre realized that he had been washed up into a cave tunnel, and that the stars were luminescent glowworms winking in and out.

How had he ended up here, when he had just been sinking, drowning? *Where* was here?

He vaguely recalled a flash of white and the feel of being carried…

Cold, the air was so cold. He couldn't stop shaking.

Clutching his dripping coat closer, he followed the tunnel, stumbling over a flooring of pebbles and rocks smoothed by the shallow stream. The farther he walked, the lighter the tunnel became, and hope filled him that he might soon step out into daylight and be reunited with his family.

But instead of daylight, the tunnel opened into a green cavern. He rested his hand against a wall covered in moss and glowing fungi.

Strange swirls and braided patterns were carved into the cavern walls. He lifted his gaze; the patterns filled every inch of wall that he could see. The light that gave the cavern a bluish daylight was coming from the cavern floor's mossy center, and at that center stood a domed structure of white stone. The same swirl and braid motifs decorated its smooth surface, he observed as he drew near. His footsteps shuddered frigidly.

He had to get dry, find something warm to wrap up in. Perhaps whatever moss was making the structure glow could also give him warmth. His feet squelched in his soaked shoes as he climbed up the white steps to a pair of double doors. The intricate design carved and painted across them was something like a giant, pale snowflake. The design glowed strangely, as if with its own inner light.

Endre grabbed one ice-like handle and pulled.

The door groaned in protest as it opened outward, and a vacuum of air sent a chill gusting through his hair, across his scalp, and down his soggy clothes.

Beyond the door was a single wide room with a steep, domed ceiling. The white walls pulsed with light, having no source that he could see as he entered. He brushed his fingers along the stone wall but felt no warmth. He shivered again.

A strange, great object stood at the center of the grand room, and he approached with caution. Spirals and twists of wood, mixed with what appeared to be ice, rose from the floor to form legs, arms, and a chairback.

Endre drew closer. There was someone seated on the grand throne: a man who looked as ancient as the cavern itself, with his beard curling down past his toes, his skin pale and densely wrinkled, his eyebrows thick as giant moths. But strangest of all were the snowflakes and feathering frost that covered his hair and beard and blue robe garments, like embroidered ice. The man's eyes were closed, as if in a frozen sleep.

Endre hesitated, debating whether he should try and wake the man or not, and if the man was even still alive to begin with.

An object glistened in the old man's pale hands. He leaned forward carefully and saw that it was a lyre. Veins of ice carved symbols across its wood-and-ice-glazed surface.

How is the ice not melting? He reached to touch the wondrous instrument, brushing his finger across one of the strings, clear as a thread of crystal.

A bolt of electricity jolted through his finger and up his arm, making him jump backwards and shake his hand. He suddenly felt exhausted, as if all of his energy had just been sapped away, and he lowered to the floor.

Invisible weights closed his eyes, and his body gave another shudder...

"Endre."

The voice stirred him awake, and he pushed himself up off the floor.

"There is no time for you to lie there, boy."

Endre jerked his head up. The ancient man was awake and standing up from the wood-ice throne. He looked paler now, and the snowflakes on him were beginning to drip and distort.

"What do you mean, no time?" Endre asked.

"I must teach you to use the winter lyre. My time is running out, and the one meant to replace me has not come." The old man's voice was like the crunching of snow. Frost fell from his eyelashes and eyebrows. He pushed the wood-and-ice lyre into Endre's hands. "You must become the next Winter Guardian. The seasons of autumn and winter will be in your hands."

Endre rubbed his fingers along the lyre strings, smooth as ice yet flexible, and ringing with crystalline sound when he plucked one. A pool of frost formed at his feet with the sound. "The seasons? Guardian? What are you talking about? No one can control the seasons," he told the man. "What sort of strange dream am I having?"

The ancient man bent down to Endre suddenly, making him jump back a step. "Dream? You think this is a dream?" His frosted grim expression didn't match his wry chuckle. "Did you honestly think you fell off a ship into the frigid ocean during a storm and survived?"

Endre stared into his icy blue eyes then looked down at the floor and the pool of frost.

"...No..." he finally said but didn't want to admit. "It would be impossible to survive something like that."

"Exactly. You died, boy. Drowned. But because I need a successor, and you were the closest person able to take on the job, I had you brought here. You feel cold now because your deceased body is cold—but soon such cold will no longer bother you." He nodded down at the lyre. "Look, even the winter lyre has accepted you. Your heart qualifies to be the new Winter Guardian."

The man held up his hand; his fingers were turning to ice, the skin becoming clear as crystal while Endre watched. His feet and nose were doing the same. Soon, the ancient man would be nothing more than a statue of ice.

"But you must agree to accept this responsibility. I cannot force it upon you. The power must be accepted."

Endre considered the lyre in his hands, thumbing the symbols like runes of ice in its wood. This was all so surreal, and it was happening too quickly. He couldn't think. "And if I choose not to?" he asked the elder.

Ice crept up the man's arms, and his grim expression turned dark. "Then the seasons will be out of balance and will lose control. The Earth and those who live here will suffer great natural disasters, and much of the world will perish."

Endre swallowed. "I couldn't let something like that happen…"

"The job of a Season Guardian is vital." The ancient man nodded, his neck above the blue robe collar shifting into ice.

"Wait! Are you dying? You can't! I don't know *what* to do, or *how* to do it!" Endre pleaded with him.

"Learn from the Summer Guardian," the old man said, his voice becoming more broken by the second. "I had wanted to teach you, but it seems that my time is up. The lyre will respond to your feelings, so you must hold it close. The rest I am certain you will figure out on your own. But remember…you cannot let a human see you." Ice began creeping over the ancient man's cheeks and light-gray beard. "Glamor will keep you hidden from human sight. It is better that way…less painful."

"But why?" Endre asked desperately.

"Do you accept the role of Winter Guardian?" the elder

asked, just as the ice was crusting over the surface of his eyes.

"…Yes, I accept," Endre forced himself to say.

The air rustled around them, and a current of snowflakes departed from the old man to strike into Endre's chest, filling him with a cold energy and new life. Frost crept across his skin and clothes like icy lace, and snowflakes stuck to his hair. The tips of his ears grew pointed like the fae, and power swirled around the winter lyre.

"You will carry on the title of Frost—your new name," the elder managed to say.

Endre watched as, within the final second, the man became a solid statue of clear ice, all color drained away. And the large room fell quiet, but for a swirling winter breeze.

Endre landed on the snow-covered ground, as quietly as he could, near the house's wide living room window. He pressed his back to the brick wall, gathered courage within himself, and then turned to peer around the wooden frame and through the glass.

There was Ada, sitting on the rug before the fireplace, a pair of knitting needles moving in her hands as she worked to make what appeared to be a scarf. She looked…older, just a little bit.

Mother and Father were on the red sofa, near the Christmas tree decorated with colorful garlands and candles and small toys. He recognized the little wooden snowflake he had made, dangling on a high branch. Father was reading them a story, as he often did on long winter nights.

Endre watched his family until they tired and went to bed.

The next day, when the sky was fading into twilight, and Ada was finishing up a snowman in the front yard, Endre came again.

He stood before her in the snow, while she wrapped her black scarf around the snowman's neck.

She really had changed. Ada was older, even though to him it felt like only months had passed since they were on the steamship.

He slowly let the cloak of glamor around him fall away, and he waited for her gaze to latch onto him. When it did, she stilled, and her face turned pale with fright.

"Ada, it's me. I'm back. I wanted you to know that I'm all right, so you wouldn't feel guilty anymore," he began to explain to her.

Ada straightened slowly, her lower lip quivering, and she moved several steps backwards, stumbling away from him. "...A ghost..." she murmured, voice trembling with fear. "Mum...Dad!"

"Wait, Ada. I'm not a ghost! I'm really here—"

But Ada ran to the door, nearly falling on a patch of ice, and was gone before he could touch her hand. He could hear her panicked voice inside the house.

He shook his head. Of course she would think he was a ghost. Years had passed since he fell to his death, and he hadn't aged a single day. What was he thinking? He was no longer a simple human.

"You cannot let a human see you... It is better that way...less painful." He recalled the ancient Guardian's words.

"Ada...Mum, Dad...I miss you," he whispered, his breath making fog crystals in the air. And with that, he left.

Years flew by as Frost traveled the northern and southern hemispheres, bringing with him autumn and winter. At the stroke of his lyre and brush of his fingers, leaves shed their green for colorful ruby, gold, and brilliant orange. Crops yielded their harvest, and orchards brimmed with apple cider. And at his call, the winter sprites helped him to spread the early frost and bring forth clouds heavy laden with snow.

More than a century passed, and Endre Frost felt the steep toll of being in the world yet not being a part of it, of seeing families spend the holidays together, knowing that he could never do the same. He worked alone, lived alone, and time made his soul grow callous.

He longed to end the Guardian work, to quit and let his soul be released, to be free and enter rest in Heaven's land, to be with his family again.

Life was no longer worth living.

And soon, all he could think of was how to put an end to it…

But for that, he would need a replacement.

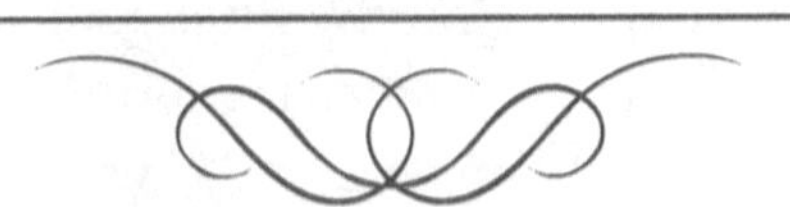

"NORAH, HURRY UP WITH THOSE noodles!" shouted the manager.

The fast-food place was busier than usual, and Norah hurried to scoop a portion of ramen noodles into a plastic bowl, quickly sprinkling on some seasoning and freezer-burned diced vegetables.

"Here's your order, sir, one bowl of fast ramen and a large soda," she said, and handed him a large soda cup. "Enjoy your meal, and please come back to The Fast Noodle soon for our weekly specials." She repeated the restaurant's line of script, and the man didn't give her so much as a half-smile.

Norah turned to serve the next customer, forcing her aching facial muscles to show them a smile.

When her shift finally came to an end for the day, she gathered her coat and scarf. Manager Jeff called after her on her way out.

"Make a brighter smile tomorrow, yes?" He pinched his cheeks, pulling his smile wider in demonstration. As an immigrant from Japan, customer service meant everything to him. She admired his determined spirit and positive attitude, even if she couldn't keep a constant smile on her own face the way he did, especially towards rude customers who just wanted to boss her around.

Norah gave a weak laugh and turned to the glass door, shoving the heavy weight open to a blast of cold air.

Stuffing her chilled hands in her coat pockets, she made the walk from South Main Street to Rund Middle School. She halted at a chain-link fence and watched as two soccer teams were battling it out.

Her little brother passed the ball to a teammate, who then kicked it into the net, scoring the final goal. The number of their total goals against the other team ultimately fell short, though. Norah watched Tim shrug on his coat and shuffle out the fence gate glumly. With winter coming, his soccer games were at an end, for now. She greeted him with a head pat, ruffling his hair, as brown as her own. "Nice job out there."

Tim made a pouty face, pretending not to like her show of affection, though he secretly smiled when he thought she wasn't looking. "You got all your stuff?" she asked, and he nodded.

She rubbed his shoulder, and they began their walk home, with the sun already setting behind them. They made their way up the streets. Some of the trees were still pretty colors, maples glowing golden or sunburst orange. But the frost would be on its way soon, and the splendor of autumn would fade quickly into winter. Not that Norah minded much. Growing up in New Hampshire, you get used to snow, and find ways of living alongside it.

The green turret became visible first, rising above a large white birch, and then the rest of the house emerged—their very old house, which had been built sometime during the 1800s. A pretty piece of history, and a pain in the butt to live in.

Norah plodded up the rickety steps to the porch. "Scrape the dirt off your shoes," she reminded Tim, while unlocking and shoving open the paneled door. She hurried to the thermostat, turning the temp up to get the furnace going. Heating oil was expensive, so when no one was in the house, they kept the stat low.

The old furnace rumbled and shuddered itself awake below in the basement, and they exchanged their shoes for thick socks. Tim headed for a big bowl of muddy buddies, snatching it from the counter and bringing it into the connected living room to munch and watch TV. Norah grabbed a handful as he passed by her, stuffing the sweet snack into her mouth.

Her phone dinged. She looked: it was a text from Scott, a classmate.

For the past two weeks, the guy had been flirting with her via texts, acting like they should date. But just yesterday, out of the blue, he told her he wasn't ready for a relationship.

Uh… Why flirt with a girl if you were *never* planning on dating her?

Jerk.

Now, his text came to inform her that he would be dating one of her friends. He was letting her know ahead of time, as his way of working on being a more open and honest person.

Whatever.

Just as Tim positioned himself on the worn, blue sofa and pressed the TV remote button, the front door burst open and a frigid gust of air blew through the rooms.

"*Shoot*, this place is cold!"

Norah winced and hunched her shoulders at the man's voice, followed on his heels by Mom as she shook off the cold and carried a bag of groceries over to the kitchen table.

"It gets worse—just wait until full-on winter's here," Norah muttered.

The man shrugged off his expensive wool coat and plaid scarf but left his shoes on. "Keep the thermostat up, you little rat. Are you trying to freeze me out of here?" He swore under his breath, shoes leaving wet marks on the old wood flooring as he veered into the living room and took Tim's spot on the sofa for himself, snatching away the remote from him. Tim shied away and moved towards Norah.

Bob was by far the worst guy Mom had ever dated, and the wealthiest—an arrogant insurance agent, who wrote policies worth seven figures.

"Little rats want to be out in the cold? Is that it? I can throw their beds out in the street if that'd make them happy—it's plenty cold out there!" Bob griped.

"Oh Bob, don't get a temper," her mom cooed, perching on the sofa back behind him. "If we have a little help with the heating expenses, we can keep it nice and toasty in here for you." She drew a finger down his nose and tapped the very tip playfully.

Bob chuckled, wrapping an arm around her waist.

Norah wanted to gag. Tim nearly did, turning away with the muddy buddies bowl hugged against his chest. They each grabbed a few more snacks and hurried up the creaking staircase to hide away for the rest of the night.

In her bedroom upstairs, Norah stood akimbo before a white bookcase, scanning the colorful rows of book spines before choosing one: an art book about watercolor techniques, which she had yet to read. Tucking the book under her arm, and holding a box of cheese chips in her other hand, she tiptoed across the squeaky upstairs hallway over to a door at the very end. It opened to a set of narrow stairs leading up into a small, circular room: the top of the turret, shaped like a mini tower. It was carpeted and cozy, and was her favorite place to read.

She grabbed a large pillow from the pile and made a comfy place beside the bay windows which ran the length of the round room. Night had already fallen, and streetlights turned the neighboring houses and trees into stark silhouettes. She struggled to see a few pinpoints of light in the sky, planets or stars large enough to cut through the city light. Concord wasn't a big city; there were no soaring buildings or anything like in Boston, but instead had a more rural feel to it, with farms and woodlands nearby.

The view from here was almost three stories up and made her feel like she was a bird perched in the tree branches just beyond the glass. She spotted two boys riding skateboards down the street below, out front, and making a ruckus. That sent the neighbor's dog up the street into a barking frenzy. The annoying, high-pitched yaps were then joined by other dogs around the area, and the entire neighborhood was soon filled with a headache-inducing cacophony.

Norah turned on her phone's playlist, drowning out the insane animals with a soft jazz.

A cold draft tickled her nose. She plopped the book and chips box down and grabbed up a roll of duct-tape. Her fingers felt along the window frames until they hit cool air seeping in from the lower right side. The tape screeched as she unrolled a long strand and stuck it along where window met wall. There were tons of drafty spots in the old house, and the cheapest way to fix them was tape. Drafty gaps also meant perfect places for bugs to sneak indoors. She found another long-legged spider down where the carpet met wall, and grabbed up her hand vacuum, sucking it up.

Finally, she sat down and rested against the pillow, thumbing through pages of artwork with one hand, while munching cheese chips with the other. She coughed, wishing she had remembered to bring a water bottle.

She let her head rest back against the edge of the window frame. Her gaze traced along the old wall, uneven lines and bumps of plaster underneath the off-white paint. One patch resembled the outline of a little sailboat.

The artbook's next page, when she turned it, showed and described techniques for painting snow and ice. There was a pretty depiction of icicles, as an example, and then several versions of Jack Frost. Most featured him with white hair and carrying an ice-making staff. She paused on the page, squinting and munching.

"His hair isn't white. It's black," she said to no one.

She tilted her head against the wall to peer out the window, looking to the powerlines that ran high along the street. A flock of pigeons were huddled there for warmth, like dark blobs in the night. But she had seen something else on the powerlines, once—walking across the wires with unearthly ease and grace. Ice had formed with every footstep that he took, spreading from his shoes outward, like magic.

In the darkness of midnight, years ago, ten-year-old Norah had woken in tears from a nightmare, and then, from her bed, she had seen *him* through the window, striding across the powerlines. The details were fuzzy now, but she remembered his hair being dark, and the snowflakes that peppered it sparkling like jewels. A swirl of frost had formed along the window as he passed by.

Jack Frost, or a creepy stalker who happened to be a tightrope walker?

Dream, or eerie real phenomenon?

Norah fingered the page, then propped her head back with a sigh. "I guess I'll never know."

"What do you mean, we have to be packed and ready to leave by tomorrow morning?" Norah tried not to let her temper rise across the phone, holding it to her cheek as she walked home from The Fast Noodle. "You're dumping us on Aunt Karin again, aren't you?"

Not that she minded being with her aunt. But the way her mom could just carelessly toss them away at someone else irked her.

"Is that so wrong? You like Portsmouth. I'm sure you'll have fun. Me and Bob just need some alone time together," said Mom's voice.

Norah tried not to vomit her lunch. "Ugh, why do you even like him?"

"Relationships aren't always about love, Norah. He has the means to provide us with a comfortable life, and when you're older, you'll see that *that's* what really matters."

Norah gritted her teeth at the phone. "In other words, he's your moneybag."

She could sense her mom's irritation from across the radio waves.

Norah continued, "He might provide for *you*, but as soon as I'm able, I'm getting my own place—and taking Tim with me."

"Don't you start being all smarty with me, young lady—"

Norah ended the call and made a face.

She would get a better job—as soon as she turned eighteen. And they would never have to deal with Mom or another Bob ever again!

Once home, Norah hurried to her room and busied herself packing a duffel bag and getting Tim ready. When morning dawned, she was up and making Tim get dressed before

Aunt Karin's car rolled up the street.

Despite the slang term sound of her name, Karin had rosy cheeks and was one of those huggable people you couldn't help but like. At the front door, she wrapped both of them in a bear hug. "Here're my favorite niece and nephew!" she said, rocking them back and forth in her thick arms before finally releasing them. "Who wants breakfast at Tucks?"

Tim hopped up and down, "Me me me!"

Norah grinned. "That'd be perfect."

Mom looked away, disgruntled. She never did like how much they loved Karin, nor that Karin believed in a Creator, God, and had taught them to believe the same. "Don't spoil them," she muttered.

"Of course, I won't. It's just a bit of food, that's all," Karin said, then winked at Tim, who muffled a giggle.

Once their bags were in the car, they headed off for the world's best ever breakfast of pancakes and waffles. Norah ate almost as much as Tim, both of them eating as if they had just come out of a famine.

She dozed off, once back in the car, and woke up when they drove over the highway bridge into Portsmouth, a bustling seacoast city. The Piscataqua River sparkled in the sun, and a strong salty breeze blew, tearing at the remaining autumn leaves on the trees.

Aunt Karin's apartment in the city was small; Norah and her brother had to share a room, but it was a breath of fresh air away from home. They spent the rest of the day touring downtown, sight-seeing old buildings, strolling brick pathways, and exploring boutiques filled with unique items.

Norah tried on fancy feathered hats and gloves from a quaint British boutique, and Tim gawked over an ancient fossil collection inside a crystals & gems shop. A décor and candle store on the next street corner caught her eye, but Tim wanted to go get ice cream next.

They ended the day with scoops of gelato and sat on a lattice bench in Market Square, watching the sun go down beyond the peaked rooftops. The white North Church steeple, rising above the square, sounded out the hour.

"I don't know about you, but I'm exhausted!" said Aunt Karin, tossing away her finished gelato cup. "Time for some dinner! Though we went backwards and had dessert first." She chuckled merrily.

Tim laughed, with some gelato smeared on his nose.

Later, after eating a seafood meal of lobster rolls and fish and chips, a chill in the air made Norah button her coat up higher. She was following Karin and Tim along the quaint street back towards the apartments, when she hesitated and asked, "Aunt, can I stop in one last shop? You don't have to wait for me. I know where you live."

Karin considered before nodding. "Mm, okay. But don't take too long; it's already dark, now that the days are shorter and all."

Norah waved and then hurried back to the candle shop—still open. Inside, it was like stepping into an eclectic world of dangling candles, books, ornaments, and handmade home décor. She sniff-tested a row of essential oils and candles, and grinned at the metal garden frogs crafted into different yoga positions.

A colorful green book of faeries begged her to thumb through its pages of art depictions—they were the cute, mischievous sort of faeries who lived in disguise among plants and who helped to bring change to the seasons. One faery was hiding among autumn leaves and causing the tree's prickly seedpods to fall; he wore a yellow hat and a merry smirk. For a lover of fantasy artwork, like herself, the book was a found treasure.

After purchasing the book, Norah stepped back outdoors into the cold, bag in hand. White lights were on along the streets. She took a moment to pause and soak in the wonder of what a world with faeries might look like. Perhaps the white lights were really the glowing berries that a faery had picked, and the frost on the ground might be delicate threads of faery lace.

She turned in place at Market Square, breathing in the scenery and letting her imagination run wild.

"Hey, wait for me!" a kid shouted to his friends, a ways from where she stood. A patch of ice appeared suddenly, and the kid tripped and fell. The other boys started laughing, until more ice appeared and made them all tumble down like dominoes.

They made a ruckus getting back on their feet.

Norah cocked her head. The shop windows were covered in frost, even though it wasn't yet fully winter, and there came a sound of quiet laughter from somewhere.

She slowly lifted her gaze to the large tree beside her in the square, where the hushed laughter sounded to be coming from.

A teenage boy was crouched on a long branch, with his feet perfectly balanced, and he chuckled at the fallen kids. She was about to scold him for laughing, when a row of icicles suddenly crept up the branch behind him. A stringed instrument glowed in his hand, and when he plucked a string, frost vined up every branch of the tree and crystalized over every leaf. Where his feet stepped, icicles dripped down the bark.

The tree didn't groan or make a sound, as if his weight were nothing. His collared, long black coat made him hard to pick out in the dark; even the scarf around his neck was black. His head turned suddenly, and he noticed her staring.

The boy stared back at her from his perch, then he glanced behind him, as if trying to spot whatever she must be looking at. Finding nothing, however, he tilted his head this way and that and then hopped over to a branch on his left. Norah's gaze followed him, even though his land on the bark didn't make a stir.

He crouched and peered down at her, leaning out of the tree.

Her gaze stayed locked onto him.

Carefully, he lifted his hand and waved it.

She slowly waved back.

His eyes shot wide open, as if he'd been hit over the head with shock. "You can…see me?" he asked.

Norah was about to comment how stupid a question that was. Couldn't everyone see him? But then she noticed his ears were pointed and that snowflakes dotted his thick, black hair, their delicate ice not melting. Lacy frost and more snowflakes trailed up his arms and across the shoulders and breast of his coat, like splashes of frosty paint. The irises of his eyes—a deep midnight blue—were rimmed in white frost.

Norah's mouth hung open for a moment. Then she finally said, "You're a faery."

The boy's gaze narrowed at her. "Not quite."

"A vampire."

"Never mind, just stick with faery." He frowned. "But how can you see me through my glamour?"

Norah tilted her head. "What do you mean? *Are* you a faery?" she asked, feeling like this must be some sort of strange dream.

The boy hopped down out of the tree; he wasn't much older than her. Where his shoes landed on the brick, swirls of frost spread out.

"Humans who can see us are rare," he stated, circling her and studying her like she was some mysterious artifact. She self-consciously smoothed her hair with a hand.

"You didn't answer my question," she tried again.

He fingered the scarf around his neck and halted in place.

"I used to be human, like you. But now, I'm the Winter Guardian. You can call me Frost."

Her face lit up. "Jack Frost!"

"*That* was the first Guardian. I'm Endre Frost." He pulled out a lyre from his coat, a beautiful thing made of wood and ice, and she reached out to touch it, without thinking.

"Are you curious?" he asked her. "Perhaps you can make the winter lyre sing?"

He held the instrument out for her, and she brushed her fingers across the crystal-like strings. They rang like a clear harp, and a swirl of snowflakes blew around her ankles.

Her mouth fell open. "It's beautiful...like magic," she breathed.

Frost's lips rose in a small smirk before quickly switching over to a smile. "It's more of a necessary power used to help run the world, rather than magic," he said.

Norah held her hands to her cheeks. "I can't believe this is real. How long have you been a Guardian? I'm almost eighteen, and you only look a year older than me," she said.

"Hey, it took me over a hundred years to finally look this old. Guardians age slowly, you know." He tucked the lyre back inside his coat, mock frowning.

"Really?" Norah ran her wide gaze over him.

"Listen, um— What was your name?"

"Norah."

"Norah, I have work to do. But maybe we can meet up again later? I'll show you more of what I can do, if you like. Where do you live?"

"Uh, in Concord." She had trouble thinking. "West Street."

Frost nodded, the movement shifting his snowflake-peppered bangs. "Until next time, then." He launched into the air, ice crystals glittering behind him. He waved to her, floating above the North Church's white steeple, before disappearing over the slate rooftops.

Norah stared long at the spot, before shaking herself back to her senses.

Were real faeries to be trusted? Should she be so eager to meet with him again?

But the wonder and magic of it all, the hope for new possibilities in her dreary life...she couldn't resist it. She hurried with her shopping bag back to Aunt Karin's apartment.

3

Frost watched from a rooftop perch as the human girl hurried away down the street. He tipped his face up to the cloudy night sky and closed his eyes.

At last, his prayers had been answered. For so long, he had roamed the Earth, tending to autumn and winter, watching from a distance as landscapes changed, as people changed, as corruption won and much of the good in the world was lost…

He was tired. Tired of living without really living, of watching humans waste their time away and constantly complain. Tired of…everything.

Now, there was a chance for him to move on from this life, to die and reunite with his family in Heaven's realm. His lonely journey could finally come to an end.

Only a rare human unaffected by the Guardian glamour could take his place. Such humans were an unexplained phenomenon and difficult to find. He would have to train her, and make sure that her heart qualified for the job. Only then could he be free.

But the girl, Norah, would have to willingly accept the Winter Guardian position—and that was something no sane person would do. So, he would have to trick her into accepting, somehow.

Frost lifted into the sky. With a strum on the winter lyre, a frigid wind ran through Portsmouth, freezing every patch of moisture into ice. He flew westward, carrying the wind in his wake over the inlets and salt marshes.

A sudden loud chime rang in his ears, like a large crystal bell, and he paused mid-flight. He still had much of New Hampshire to cover, but the scheduled meeting could not be ignored.

He strummed the last lyre string, and a winter sprite appeared and flew to him. "Gather the others and finish the rest of this while I'm gone," he told the creature, indicating with a wave the landscape westward.

The sprite nodded its delicate ice head.

Frost departed, curving his flight up through the many layers of clouds and into Earth's atmosphere…

When Frost entered the grand hall, his shoes made a light *tap-tap* sound across the glass-like floor tiles. The transparent floor showed stars and the curve of Earth's surface below. The left side of the hall was made up of columns of ice and dangling icicles, mixed with colorful patches of bright autumn leaves, purple grapes, gourds and pumpkins. The right side of the hall contained columns of tree bark and dangling vines, nuts and berries, and a myriad of tropical flowers and cherry blossoms.

The Hall of Seasons, it was named, hovering high above the British Isles, where the Nymph of Seasons dwelled. And where Frost had to give his seasonal reports.

He halted before the vacant marble-and-glass throne and stood himself off to the side, leaning against one of the ice columns and pocketing his hands.

"So, we meet again, my young pupil."

Frost turned his face to the young man coming down the hall with a pep in his step, his appearance not much older than Frost, though he had far more Guardian experience, and stood slightly taller.

Jules Leaf. His auburn hair was peppered with vine leaves, and threads of moss wove up his bare arms and shoulders and over his maroon cloak; various fern mosses covered his bare feet. The playful glint in his clay-colored eyes slid over to Frost.

"Stop calling me your pupil. The only thing you did was showed me a few ropes of the Guardian job, nothing more," Frost snapped.

"Ouch. Touchy today, aren't we?" Leaf tapped the wooden Summer Guardian flute against his shoulder.

"If you want to unsour my mood, then let me bring winter to Florida, for a change."

"Florida?" Leaf exclaimed. "Are you crazy? Why not ask for the whole Gulf of Mexico, while you're at it?" He shook his head, the vines in his hair swishing. "Some places are meant to stay perpetually hot, Frost, no matter what *you* may prefer."

"Children in Florida would like to see a little snow. What's so wrong with that?"

"You'll ruin the flora and the entire ecosystem, that's what! Stay out of my summer domain, Snowflake."

A dangerous glint lit in Frost's eye at the nickname.

"You want to talk about domains?" He faced Leaf sourly.

"What about that hot day you brought to Maine right in the *middle* of February? Hot days should never exist in the north in *February*!"

"It was an accident." Leaf's mouth took on a pout. "My bad mood changed the weather when I was passing through, that's all."

"That's all?" Frost repeated furiously and took a step forward.

"Well, you've made it snow on Easter multiple times," Leaf retorted and also took a step forward, making a face at him. "Easter, you know, the *spring* holiday."

The two Season Guardians stared each other down for one drawn moment, neither one backing away, not even so much as blinking. Then, the far door opened and the Nymph of Seasons entered the hall, gliding over to the throne.

She moved with fluid grace, her body and flowing dress the texture and translucency of water. White birch antlers rose around her head, and on them, pink flower buds bloomed and faded in a continuous cycle, making a constant rain of petals fall about her shoulders.

The Guardians broke their staring match and put space between themselves, standing at attention.

"How fares the seasonal change this year?" she asked them both. Her voice like a rippling stream carried through the hall.

Leaf spoke up first, with a miffed glance his way. "The transition of spring to summer in the southern hemisphere is going beautifully well. You should see the relief and joy on people's faces, eager to have the cold and drear done away with."

Frost didn't miss the jibe. "The transition of autumn to winter is progressing. Families are benefiting from spending more time together as the weather chills," he announced.

Leaf rolled his head to the side and barked a laugh. "Sure they are. Stuck indoors all day, eating their emotions away and becoming TV zombies."

"They do that during the summer too, now," Frost jabbed back.

The Nymph of Seasons raised a liquid hand to pause them. "Have you discussed how far winter's boundary will reach this year?" she asked.

They glanced hostilely at one another.

"I say the lower lands, like Florida, should be allowed some snow," said Frost.

Leaf crossed his sun-tanned arms. "And I say that's utterly ridiculous. Think of how many flowers would die?"

Frost rolled his eyes to the side. "Who cares about flowers? They have those all year long. But snow—now, that'd be a rare treat for people."

"You just want to kill the gardens and ruin the roads in my domain!" Leaf pointed at him accusingly. "You know very good and well how poorly equipped southerners are for winter."

"Oh, my bad. I forgot that a few centimeters of snow is enough to shut down the entire state." Frost smirked, hands up in mock defense.

Leaf shook his head and gave a dry laugh. "Smirk all you like, but you northerners are such crybabies, you can't even breathe if the air gets above 80 degrees Fahrenheit."

"My seasons have the best holidays and food," Frost growled.

Leaf rolled his shoulders and lifted his chin. "At least *my* seasons don't give people frostbite or diabetes."

Their glares intensified, as if by sheer willpower they might be able to burn a hole through the other's head.

"Enough." The Nymph's cool voice silenced them, and they hastily bowed their heads.

"Forgive me," they each muttered to her, cutting glares at one another.

"Every year is the same," said the Nymph of Seasons, exasperation in her voice. "You cannot continue in this manner. The Season Guardians must work together, in perfect harmony, in order for the seasons to be stable. That is how our Creator designed it to be." The flowers on her antlers turned an angry red, and Leaf swallowed. "I cannot allow this behavior to persist. From henceforth, you are both to share the same living quarters and learn to—as the humans say—*get along*," she ordered.

Frost stared at her in shock. "The same…"

"…living quarters?" finished Leaf.

"If you can learn to share a house and live in harmony, then you can learn to share the seasons, as well," she surmised, and with a tone that would not allow any argument from them. "There is a condo in Boston, purchased with the Season Guardian inheritance funds. You will live there for one entire year. Being among humans should also force you to control yourselves and behave more properly."

Twin cardkeys materialized in the air before Frost and Leaf. They each took one gingerly, as if the keys might bite.

"Go, and make your plans for winter," the Nymph said, and with a wave of her arm, she vanished from the hall.

Uncomfortable silence ensued.

"Well." Leaf tossed the key in his hand. "Time to go and see my new living nightmare."

"*Our* living nightmare," Frost corrected.

NORAH SHOOK HER HEAD TO JOSTLE her brain. Last night, did she really tell a strange faery where she lived?

A cold shudder ran up her spine.

But, oh my, he had been gorgeous to look at. Far better than any Jack Frost Hollywood could ever come up with. Luscious black hair, perfect fair skin, all of him dotted in glittery snowflakes, and tendrils of frost lacing his perfectly deep blue eyes…

She shook herself again. Small snowflakes were drifting from the cumulous clouds overhead. She watched them drift down onto the calm waters of the docks and onto the yachts and sailboats tied there. She stood at the chain-link fence barrier for a while, then moved on towards the old

Sheafe Warehouse and the wooden pier jutting out across the slow waves.

"How long does it take to order a take-out breakfast?" she mumbled. Maybe Aunt Karin was stuck in a long line at the coffee shop? It felt like she'd been waiting for her for over an hour. Poor Tim was probably starving back at the apartment. Norah would have offered to make breakfast, but her aunt didn't have much in the way of groceries and wanted to bring them a special breakfast from her favorite café and bakery.

Norah crossed the dirt path and onto the boards of the pier. The ground here sloped down to a small, rock-and-sand stretch of beach on either side. She would have continued down to the pier's end, but a green object bobbing in the water caught her attention.

Squinting at it, she squeaked when she realized the *object* had a pair of eyes.

The green *thing* lifted itself halfway out of the water. It was a girl, perhaps several years older than herself, with green hair the color of seaweed and a strange full-body swimsuit.

"What the— You're going swimming at this time of year?" Norah exclaimed over the pier rails. "I mean, it *is* less crowded in the winter. But still."

The girl's green eyes shifted up to her. Her lips parted and her expression turned curious. "You noticed me?" she asked quietly. Then the strange girl raised her voice, "There's no need for you to worry about my wellbeing. I have on a…wetsuit, I believe they call it. The water isn't so cold today, either."

Norah blinked. "Uh, if you say so."

"Do you live in this city?" asked the girl.

"No, I'm in Concord. But it might be nice to live here on the coast, someday. There's a lot more going on out here—things to do, things to get involved in. I'd like to join an art organization, make and sell artwork."

"Artwork…" The girl held her gaze. "What things are you making?"

Norah shrugged her shoulders. "Nothing right now. Just going to school and working at a fast-food place."

"Fast food? How interesting. Does the food move very fast?"

Norah paused and got an odd feeling.

No, the girl couldn't be a faery; she couldn't keep letting her imagination run wild after that encounter last night. Maybe the girl was trying to make a joke—and was clearly very bad at it.

"Sure, that's the whole point," Norah went along with it.

"Fascinating." The girl seemed to marvel at the statement. "I am Selk. What are you called?"

"Uh, Norah."

That was a strange way of asking someone's name.

"Norah, you have an interesting life."

Norah's brow wrinkled. "Okay, thanks, I guess. But I'm sure yours is better than mine."

Selk smiled, her lips a purplish hue. "Show me the fast food when we meet next," she said, and with that, her body lowered and she vanished beneath the gray waves.

Norah looked about, but no green head popped up for air anywhere. She was pretty sure Selk wasn't wearing a diving tank.

"Well…that was strange."

"Norah, I've been trying to find you!"

Norah turned around, and there came Aunt Karin towards the pier, coffees and breakfast bags in hand.

She offered a sheepish smile. "You know me, I can't keep still and not go off exploring."

Her aunt nodded with a look that said *Obviously*. "Come help me carry all this!"

Norah trotted across the boards, glancing back one last time.

The strange girl was still nowhere to be seen.

Back home in Concord after the weekend, Norah finished her online application to Dartmouth College, hoping to get into their Arts program.

"There, done! If I'm accepted, I'll be on my way towards a fine arts degree!" she cheered from the kitchen table.

Tim peeked over the couch at her while watching TV. "Shouldn't you wait until summer to start worrying about all that?" His question crossed the kitchen to her ears.

"It's never too early to start!" Norah insisted. "And besides, for a popular college like this one, I need *every* head start I can get. So many people apply there, and only the very best make it in."

"Better start on plan B, then," shot Tim.

She threw a crumpled paper at him.

He grinned, ducking. "I just meant in case you don't get any of the scholarships you applied for."

"Wow, you're such a boost of encouragement." She stuck out her tongue.

But her annoying little brother was right. If she didn't get some big scholarships, she would have no hope of affording college—and no hope of getting a decent paying job and an apartment, so they could finally be free.

The squeal of a car pulled up to the house. They knew what that meant.

Both she and Tim grabbed food and raced each other upstairs, before Bob could enter the door and be a jerk towards them again.

In her room, Norah perched her elbows on the windowsill and absently watched the sunset colors shift, the sun's rays struggling to break through an overcast sky.

She *had* to get an arts degree. Dartmouth College had to accept her application. Art was the one thing she was good at, the one thing she knew she could make a decent living off of. With a good job, her and Tim's escape from this place would be soon. Failure was *not* an option.

After a while of staring at nothing and thinking, the powerlines above her house began to grow little icicles.

She watched them curiously, until a shape came into view: a person walking gracefully across the lines, his footsteps light as a feather.

Frost.

Her lips involuntarily stretched into a small grin. She unlatched the window and screen, hoisting both up, the wood creaking with age. "Frost, you came!" she said.

Hands stuffed in his black coat pockets, he looked down at her, the edges of his scarf swaying in a faint breeze. "Of course. I said we would meet again, didn't I?"

He halted at the end of the powerline, bent into a crouch, and held out his hand for her. She stared at his palm, his fair skin glistening. "How long are you going to stare at it?" he said with an edge. "It's a hand."

She shook herself mentally and climbed out into a sitting position on the sill, then took his hand. "How am I supposed to—?" she began, but cut off when he took flight and his hand pulled her up into the air with him.

Her legs flailed for the first few panicky seconds, but he drew her close and wrapped his arm around her waist, sending a chill running through her. The shoe of her left foot stood balanced on top of his right shoe.

The ground moved below them: roofs, snow-speckled trees and patches of fallen leaves. When a park and gazebo drew near, Frost lowered their flight.

"—to get down," Norah finished the sentence to herself, as her shoes crunched down upon the melting snow and Frost released her, landing a few feet away. She looked about, but no one else was around the park at this late hour.

From his coat, Frost pulled out the winter lyre, the ice runes engraved in the wood seeming to glow with their own inner light. "You must be used to winter, growing up here. I shouldn't have been surprised that a special human like you would be born in this area," he said.

"Can other people really not see you?" she questioned.

"Not unless I want them to," was all the answer he gave. He stroked one finger down the lyre's strings, and the ground—both bare and snow-patched—became encased in a thick layer of ice that spread with a crackling sound.

He strummed a high cord next, and Norah felt her shoes lift—skates made of ice appearing beneath them, and before she knew it, she was sliding.

"W-whoa!" Norah pinwheeled her arms to keep her balance.

Frost caught her shoulders, turning her in place to face him. He smiled and took her hands in his, though that smile didn't seem to quite reach his midnight eyes.

"With ice, I can create anything—anything your imagination can dream up," he told her.

"Really? Can you make me a giant chocolate cake and a pet Pegasus?"

Frost's expression faltered, as if unsure whether to take her seriously or not. She let out a laugh and said, "I'm just teasing. I know what you meant."

He let himself laugh a little, too. "You're an interesting girl, Norah." He began to skate backwards, pulling her forward along with him. He moved as if he didn't need to see behind him, skating around the gazebo, weaving between maple trees. She clung to his cold hands, using his balance. His scarf waved about, framing his perfect cheekbones. The frosty edges around his irises seemed to glow in the twilight, and the moon came out from behind the clouds.

He released her suddenly, and she panicked, tilting backwards and forwards, sliding across an open stretch of the park. The winter lyre sung forlorn notes, and walls of ice thrust up from the ground on either side of her, like the walls of a gorge. She skated between them, running her fingers along the cold, slick surfaces.

On the other side of the ice walls, a pavilion of ice materialized, and she was headed straight into one of its columns.

Frost caught her arm and veered her to the side, just in time. "Got you." He skated her slowly beneath the pavilion, icicles dangling from the roof's edges like sparkling diamonds all around them.

Her mouth hung open in awe. "It's beautiful..." she said, then glanced over at him. Her cheeks grew suddenly hot. "The way the ice sparkles in the moonlight, I mean."

"Of course." Frost slowed them to a stop, and the ice skates melted away.

She tried to calm her pulse and said, "That was fun! Thank you. You really are like a winter faery... I mean, I hope that isn't offensive. I'm not sure what to call you. Are there any others like you?"

His expression smoothed, unreadable. "There's a Summer Guardian. And I have winter sprites who I lend power to, to help me spread the seasons, but you can't carry a conversation with them."

"Oh... That sounds lonely," she said, then regretted it when a shadow crossed his features at her words.

"...Sometimes," he said casually. Then he put on a cheerful mask, and the lyre sang soft notes in his hands. Snowflakes drifted over the city of Concord as they watched. "But I have my own fun. I can play pranks, crash the vehicles of arrogant jerks, and travel anywhere I like."

"Travel?" Norah's interest piqued. "I would love to travel! Wow, I can't even begin to imagine what that must be like." Her smile fell a fraction, remembering the long nights of reading travel blogs and browsing through photos, wishing she could go and explore the world beyond her New England home.

"Yes, travel is a fun part of being the Winter Guardian," Frost told her, almost eagerly. He held out the lyre to her. "Here, try it. Call forth more snow for me and see if it works."

Her fingers wrapped around the curved wood and she held the instrument close, its weight surprisingly light.

"Picture in your mind what you want to create, and then let the lyre guide your fingers."

She didn't have a clue what that meant, but closed her eyes and pictured lots of snow. She touched her hand to the lyre strings and felt an invisible pull on her third finger. The pull guided her finger across three low notes and her thumb over one high note.

"Open your eyes," spoke Frost's voice near her ear. She shivered and looked.

All around them, large snowflakes fell from the sky, like a continuous rain of stars gliding down to the earth.

A *lot* of snowflake stars.

"Oh, crud!" she exclaimed. "I didn't mean to make this much snow—and it's so heavy. There are going to be a lot of angry people out plowing in the morning."

Frost barked a laugh and he glided around her. "It makes life interesting, doesn't it? It's all part of the fun."

Norah plucked the highest note, and a sudden wind blew through the park and knocked her over onto her backside. It swayed the trees, making them creak alarmingly. She pushed off her back and tried to get up. "Quick, make it stop!" She tossed the lyre to Frost.

He caught it deftly and strummed two low notes.

The wind calmed down to a breeze.

Norah tried to breathe past the thudding of her heart. "Sorry…" She wiped her cold, wet nose on her sweater sleeve. "Is all that power coming from just the lyre, then?"

Frost's snowflaked hair rustled as he shook his head. "Most of the power is my own, and the lyre helps me to channel it. But there is a portion in the lyre itself, which you can practice with."

Her brow wrinkled. "Practice?" What did he mean by that, she wondered?

Frost looked off to the side and tucked the lyre away in his coat. Was he nervous about something? "Since you can see me, I thought it would be nice to spend time with you, and let you help me with my winter work, for a while—that's what I meant."

He took her hands into his suddenly. "I'd like to spend more time with you… Can you help me not to feel lonely?"

Norah felt her face heat again. There was a loneliness behind the lacy frost and midnight blue of his eyes, but also something else. Something she couldn't quite pinpoint. And it would have made her uneasy if it weren't for his smile and the way his fingers curled around hers.

"Yes, I'd love— I mean, I'd like that, too," she replied haltingly.

He leaned forward, and she thought he might press a kiss to her lips, but he halted halfway. "Thank you. This means the world to me," he said.

In that, he sounded heartbreakingly sincere. And then, she realized they were gliding up into the air again. He held her shoulders and she stood on his feet, trying not to cling to his waist so much.

It felt like a dream, like being carried by a magical prince through falling snow-stars. Her faery prince.

He hovered before the windowsill of her room and let her down.

She climbed inside, then turned to say goodnight, but Frost was already off, flying over the rooftops.

Norah woke, a pleasant giddy feeling in her stomach. She stretched and sat up in bed.

That hadn't been a dream, right? It'd be just her luck if it was…

"What the heck!" she heard Mom's shout coming from downstairs, and using other colorful language. "How'd all this snow just happen overnight?" she exclaimed.

Norah looked out her window. The tree branches beyond were heavy with white, and people out in the street were busy shoveling, cursing, and looking very unhappy.

Norah drew her knees up to her chin. "Oops. Sorry, everybody in Concord."

5

LEAF DUMPED A BAG OF GROCERIES on the polished kitchen counter. Then he cried out in shock, "My flowers!"

Frost sauntered across the smooth floor tiles of the luxury two-story condo, the home which the Season Guardians inheritance funds had paid for. The home which the two of them were now forced by the Nymph of Seasons to share.

"What are you yelping about this early in the morning?" Frost asked lazily, sporting a close-fitted dark sweater and sipping coffee.

Leaf pointed at the vase over on the kitchen dining table. "You frosted my flowers, *again!*" he exclaimed, casting him a heated glare.

Frost turned his gaze to the vase and the white crystals that encased the flower petals and leaves. "Well, that's what I do. Don't take it personally."

As Leaf's lip began to twitch angrily, Frost indicated the green vines dangling above and around the kitchen sink window. "Why are there leaves around the sink? Do you know how tacky that looks? Every time I stand there to wash, those infernal leaves scratch across my head, ruining my hair."

Leaf crossed his arms. "Vines are a piece of art. They add tranquility and clean air to a room's atmosphere."

"Fine. I guess you won't mind if I change them to suit my taste?" Frost twisted his hand in the air, and the green vines deepened to a red autumn.

Leaf's eyes went wide. "No! How could you taint such a lovely shade of green?" His lip curled in a snarl, and he raised his right hand. The red changed back to green.

"If you want to keep it, it stays red."

"I've got news for you, ice princess. This house is half mine! And I say the vines stay green."

Tension crackled in the air between them, like a pair of stags ready to face-off with antlers lowered, and their Guardian powers sparked through the kitchen. The power struck the vines, and the leaves became a mottled red-and-green mix.

They both eyed the resulting ugliness for a moment.

"Fine, keep your plants," Frost relented. "But the floor stays ice cool." He kicked off his shoes and socks, spreading frost wherever he walked.

"*Brrr.*" Leaf rubbed his legs as if chilled, wearing only shorts and moss tendrils. He came around the counter, thick socks and moss already wrapping around his feet. "You do that anyway. You're like a walking freezer."

"And you're like a volcanic sauna," shot Frost, grabbing a

bottle of sparkling cider from the fridge, the handle freezing at his touch.

Leaf went to grab a soda and flinched at the cold, shaking his fingers to get the warmth back into them. He heated the ice away with his palm. "This is going to be a *long* year," he muttered under his breath and went over to the plush white sofa, flopping down onto it. He drank, admiring the view of Boston Harbor and the Financial District beyond the floor-to-ceiling windows of the living room space. The peach-colored horizon of dawn was painting the rooftops and glass buildings in a golden glaze.

"Maybe not," spoke Frost.

Leaf paused in his admiring and turned his head towards the adjoining sofa, where the winter guy now lounged. He lifted one auburn eyebrow at him. "Should I be concerned about what that means?"

Frost shrugged. "Not really. If anything, you'll be glad not to see my cold face anymore."

Leaf narrowed his eyes, the tiny vine leaves in his hair shifting skeptically. "That depends. What are you planning?"

Frost sipped the cider in his crystal glass, feathers of ice wrapping around the base. "I've found a candidate to become the next Winter Guardian," he said, satisfaction lining his features.

Leaf sat up so quickly that he choked on his soda. "What? You found a human who can take your place, already?"

"What do you mean *already*? It's been over a hundred years!" Frost sighed. "Don't spoil my good mood. If things work out, and she accepts the job, I'll be gone and out of your hair."

Leaf leaned back in the sofa. "Hmm. I hope this human will be far more pleasant to deal with than you've been," he mused. "How are you going to convince her to throw away her life and become a lonely wanderer, whose only bed is ice and only friends are penguins? *Ouch!*" He pulled out the icicle that Frost flung at his shoulder.

"Let *me* worry about that. She's eager enough to believe anything I tell her," said Frost, staring at the cider as he swirled the glass.

"If you say so. Well, I'm off to take my shower first! Bring the girl over sometime, so I can meet her." Leaf winked.

"Hey! Don't you turn the shower room into a steaming jungle again! Use the spare shower," shouted Frost.

But Leaf was already out of sight.

In another Boston condo, directly across from the luxury condo building, Bob stood at the wide window of his kitchen area. He'd just sent a provocative text to Norah's mom, when a flash of light caught his eye beyond the window.

It came from the flat opposite his. And when he looked more closely, there was something strange about the place: Vines dangled down one of the windows, and was it just his imagination or were they changing color from green to red and back again? He blinked several times through binoculars, and the vines now remained green.

"*Hmph.* Guess I've gotta get my eye exam soon," he mumbled. The wide balcony of the other condo looked oddly slick, too, as if covered in ice. But there was no snow or frozen water anywhere else outdoors that he could see, and his own balcony was fine.

While he stood there spying and being nosy, another window farther to the side of the flat began steaming up, and leaves crawled up over the glass, obscuring whatever was going on inside.

"What the…? Some nature-loving weirdo's living in there," Bob surmised.

He should get ready for work soon, but curiosity kept him standing there, watching.

Nothing else happened, and after a few minutes he got bored and changed out of his robe, heading off to order breakfast. He stopped at the window one last time before leaving—and halted.

The steam was gone and the leaves shriveled, all of it now replaced by large snowflakes.

He blinked and blinked.

"Must be going crazy. Too many late TV nights…"

Frost entered the shower room after Leaf, and was hit by a frothing cloud of steam. He coughed, gagging to breathe, and turned on the fan. The place was brimming with vines and flowers like a freaking volcanic jungle.

"You do this *every* time!" he shouted, regardless if the guy could hear him or not.

He swung his arm in an arc through the air, and a cold breeze forced the steam back and the droplets to crystallize. Leaves either shriveled or turned autumn red.

He grumbled a series of inarticulate words as he stepped into the glass-enclosed shower and scrubbed his hair under cold water.

Season Guardians didn't really have to take showers, or eat, or do most of the things humans did. But it was something he and Leaf still did regardless, whether it was for nostalgia's sake or to feel real and a part of the world they used to live in.

He breathed in the chill, letting water run down his face. This week would be busy: guiding a blizzard through Canada, lowering the arctic front, and then meeting up with that girl again. What was her name? Norah.

He still needed to test her, make sure if her heart qualified for the job.

When Frost came back out into the wide living room space, moss and flowers were sprouting over all the furniture and squishing underneath his toes.

"LEAF!" he shouted.

Norah ignored the notifications dinging on her phone as she marched past the school's front door columns and down the steps. She knew it was just more comments on FB about her former friend and that flirty Scott now officially dating.

Ugh.

Well, she hoped Emma and the flirt would have a wonderful relationship for a month, or however short it would last.

Norah pulled her scarf up over her chin. This week had been more chilly than normal for November, and Frost hadn't appeared to her since that day in the park. Thanksgiving had already come and gone—and what a gloomy holiday that had been, having to share it with arrogant Bob!

Maybe Frost was busy? He did say he had work to do.

Speaking of work, she jogged her way to Main Street and The Fast Noodle. The line was bursting with late-lunchers when she came in, and when Jeff spotted her, he called out and snapped his hands together repeatedly. "Norah! You late. Kitchens need extra hands; people are in food frenzy. Hurry, hurry, hurry!"

She shucked her coat off and tied on the apron, then tied her hair back and put on the ridiculous red cap.

"Laziness bad for business!" Jeff said as he passed by the kitchen door.

"*I know!*" she wanted to snap back, but got to work frying

dumplings and stirring noodle pots instead.

Freddie, the other employee sharing her shift, smirked. "Who knew a crowd of people would be so eager to eat freezer-burned veggies, huh?" he whispered to her.

Norah snorted a laugh. "Quantity over quality, I guess."

"Less gossip, more work!" Jeff's head poked in through the doorway.

"Righto." Freddie saluted.

Hours later, Norah was rubbing her sore lower back from standing for so long.

"Need a break, out front?" Freddie offered her.

She wiped her forehead with the back of her hand. "Yeah, I think I will."

The crowd had dwindled to just three people now, and they were already seated at tables. Norah stretched her arms from her spot at the cash register.

The heavy glass entrance doors squealed open, and she looked up.

A young woman, wearing a strange wetsuit and heavy coat, glanced about the place until her eyes locked with Norah's. She had green, wavy hair.

"Selk?" Norah asked tentatively.

"Ah, Norah. This is where you eat food?" Selk tilted her head, taking in the dining area, the ceiling lights, and the noise coming from the kitchen, as if she'd never seen a restaurant before—which was, you know, weird. Was she high on something?

"How about I buy you some ramen?" Norah suggested with a nervous laugh and called for the order. "Go choose a table."

"Choose?" Selk looked about, both curious and puzzled. She finally chose a seat near the room's center.

Norah brought the ramen over, and an extra cup for herself. "So, what brought you here? How'd you find me?"

"There is a great river running through Concord, but many detours through small brooks were necessary before I could reach it."

Norah blinked and sucked in her lips. "Pardon?"

River, brooks? What was this wetsuit girl talking about? "You didn't swim in the river, did you?" Norah glanced again at the wetsuit. "Uh…I mean, it hasn't frozen over yet, but do you enjoy swimming in frigid waters and that sort of thing?"

"Where is the fast-moving food? I can't seem to see it anywhere. This is the place you mentioned to me, isn't it?" Selk asked, her head turning about.

"*This* is the food." Norah indicated the ramen bowls. "They're already made, served fast. You know, that's why it's called The Fast Noodle. Fast food doesn't actually mean the food is moving." She felt weird even having to explain that.

Selk cocked her head, then stared at the food.

"The fork, see?" Norah showed her twirling her fork in the noodles and lifting them to her mouth.

Selk slowly stabbed the fork into the bowl and twirled it, slopping noodles about. She finally managed to lift and slurp up one noodle. "Mm…" She appeared to think about the taste. "More interesting than deep seaweed."

"Uh, it's not seaweed at all," said Norah. "They're noodles. Would chopsticks be easier for you? We have some."

"Noodles…noodles…" Selk swirled them around the bowl, as if studying a new form of life.

"Yeah." Norah made a funny look and tried to eat quickly, urging Selk to do the same. Once done, she stood. "I have another twenty minutes on my shift, so I'd better get back to work. But, um, come by again sometime, okay? And keep warm out there."

Selk rose and bowed her head. "Yes, I will see your face again. Thank you for the noodles fast food." She glided gracefully to the heavy door and out.

TIM OPENED THE FRONT DOOR for Norah. Now that soccer practice was over for the season, he got home before she did from work. "Mail came," he said, slinging an envelope across the kitchen table towards her.

She caught it before it tipped over the edge. "New Hampshire state…" She read the address, and realized it came from the college scholarship she'd applied for.

Her pulse quickened.

This was it. Inside the envelope was either their ticket to freedom away from Bob, or their doom by dragon fire breath. Okay, maybe she had been watching too many Middle Earth movies.

But being turned into ashes by Smaug actually sounded like a better fate than spending one more day with that guy.

"Is that...?" Tim's eyes grew wide.

She nodded slowly.

"Just rip it open, like a band-aid," he said.

She tore open the flap and pinched the letter out. "Norah Delz," she read. "We regret to inform you that..." Her voice trailed away. Tears stung her eyes before she could control them.

"Oh..." Tim's face fell.

"I failed... I wasn't good enough. Tim, I'm so sorry." She brushed her eyes, and her throat tightened.

"Nah, don't worry about it. You can just work for a year and save up money. Who needs a stupid ol' scholarship, anyway? Maybe I'll go get a job and make us a living. I can do it!" Tim brightened.

"You're too young to work, kiddo."

But even saving up money from a full year of work wouldn't be enough for Norah to pay for even just one year of college. And Tim wouldn't be old enough for college or a decent job for six more years. How much longer were they going to have to put up with Bob, or whoever Mom brought home next? How could they keep living like this, and without any decent meals? Mom rarely cooked.

She stared at the paper—the paper that had ruined her plan and doomed their future. It crumpled into a ball in her fist. Someone else had been more worthy of the scholarship than her... Where had she gone wrong?

Car wheels made a high-pitched squeal at the front of their house, and she and Tim made their way upstairs—again—her a little more sluggishly, this time. She didn't bother to turn on the light but sat in the darkness of her room and worried about the future, how she could make a better life for herself and Tim.

She needed to find a second job, somewhere, if she had any hope of saving up some sort of college fund…

A tapping on the glass made her lift her head.

Frost crouched before the windowpane, his head leaning to the side, and somehow not falling over.

She gave a start. He'd come! One good thing to happen on this dreary day, like a sudden light cutting into the darkness.

She opened the window and climbed out to his waiting arm, which wrapped around her waist as he carried her up into the sky.

"How've you been?" he asked.

"Oh, you know. Surviving life." Norah gave a mild laugh. Her arms held around his chest as he carried them over Concord.

"That doesn't sound fun," he commented.

"I'd rather not think about it. You're here, and I'm glad," she said, and she glanced sideways into his midnight gaze.

"Allow me to take your mind off your troubles, then." He flashed a grin that warmed her. "I know just the place! Hold on tight." He stretched his free arm up, and a vortex of snow formed above them.

Norah cringed apprehensively.

"You've always wanted to travel, right?" he said.

"Yeah, but what is that…?"

Norah didn't get to finish.

Frost flew straight as an arrow up into the snowy vortex. She clung to him like a panicked monkey, her hair whipping all about her face.

When they came out the other side, it was into a valley surrounded by tall mountains. Not the rounded, milder shapes like in New Hampshire, but giant death-defying peaks, their sides craggy and sharp, all steep rock and layers of snow.

"Where are we…?" she began.

"Anyone who wants to call themselves a traveler has to see the European Alps," he said simply. "It's after midnight here, but these towns never seem to sleep. Come on!"

A little town glowed below them with warm lamplights, all peaked rooftops and gables and half-timbered houses, and even an ancient church steeple. Her feet touched down on the cobblestone streets wet with half-melted snow.

"Ah, you weren't wearing shoes in your room," Frost noticed, squinting at her socks. "Guess this calls for a makeover!"

She didn't have a chance to protest as he picked her up in his arms and carried her to the nearest clothing shop.

Before she knew it, she was decked out in a thick sweater and coat, Austrian snow boots, gloves, and a white fur hat. Frost nodded approvingly, and grabbed her hand, leading her through the town's narrow streets to the square.

Christmas lights and lampposts lit up the wide space, and a tall festive Christmas tree glowed and sparkled at the center. A market of booths was spread about, selling all sorts of hand-made items. The sounds of people and energetic children brought cheer to the atmosphere.

Frost handed her a cup of hot chocolate. She savored the flavor, richer and sweeter than the cheap kind back home, and they went for a stroll. Christmas ornaments filled every booth and shop front: delicate wooden snowflakes, hand-painted rocking horses and Santas, rows and rows of different nutcrackers and smokers.

Cookies and various baked goods filled the air with sugary and savory smells. She ate a real Austrian roasted sausage, a mince pie, and almond biscuits with raspberry jelly.

"Here, you have to try the roasted chestnuts." Frost handed her a paper cone full of them.

She peeled the shells off, revealing the soft green nut underneath.

It tasted like a potato-ish treat, nicely counteracting all of the sugar she'd just been eating.

Norah halted in place, turning slowly and taking in the view of the Christmas market and decorated square, the wreaths and ribbons, and all the merry people and food. She sighed. "I could get used to this. Is there some way I could move here?" she joked.

A sly smile flashed across Frost's face. "It's easy for a Guardian," he said. "You can make your home anywhere you like!"

Their walk brought them around to a bonfire, where people were roasting sausages, potatoes, and other treats.

Norah jolted to a halt, her feet digging into the uneven street stones. The fire crackled, bits of flames waving in her vision. And smoke.

Choking smoke. Burning house. Fire licking out of the windows. Dad...

Frost tugged on her hand, but she remained frozen.

"Norah?" His brow furrowed in a question.

She pulled back, moving backwards away from the bonfire, the blaze, the deadly heat.

"What's wrong?"

She turned sharply on her heels and bolted in the opposite direction, escaping from the sight of the flames.

"Norah? Norah!" Frost chased after her.

He caught her sleeve finally when they ran into an alley. There, she slowed to a stop and covered her eyes with her gloved hands, panting.

"What happened back there?" he asked after a while, and she moved her hands down, folding her arms together and hugging herself.

"Nothing. I just...don't like fire," she mumbled, chin down against her chest.

"What?" Frost said in disbelief, as if it was ridiculous.

Maybe it *was* to other people—but not to her. "Who doesn't like fire? It keeps you warm and brings light into the cold nights. Not to mention toasted marshmallows and s'mores and… How can any human not like fire?"

Norah turned her head away to the side, blinking rapidly.

Frost watched her for a moment, his eyebrows slanted inward, displeased about something, then he tipped his face up to the starry sky. "Fine. It's time we headed back, anyway."

He wrapped his arm around her from the side, and they lifted off the ground. She shifted to hold onto him. Above the picturesque town the mountains loomed grandly, and there were more stars than any urban sky could ever hold, the Milky Way like a bright river carving through the deep.

The snowy vortex summoned by Frost swallowed them, and the landscape became Concord once again.

"Please don't think I'm not grateful," she said as Frost lowered to her window. "I had a lot of fun—more than I've had in years, actually. I like spending time with you." Her cheeks reddened from letting herself be so open, vulnerable.

Frost let her down. The scarf around him shifted in the breeze. The trails of frost along his coat arms and shoulders, and the snowflakes in his dark hair, glittered under the moonlight.

"I'll see you again, soon," was all he said, with barely a smile, before he vanished into the shadows of night.

She stood at the window for a while, her gut churning in turmoil.

Tim barged through her bedroom door suddenly, sending her pulse skyrocketing. "I need help with math again!" he stated. Then he paused, looking her up and down with narrowed eyes. "Why are you dressed for a blizzard? And those clothes look odd."

"Oh!" She glanced down at herself, then began tugging off

the hat, gloves, and boots. "I was just trying some things on for style. You know, girl fashion stuff."

Tim rolled his eyes exaggeratedly. "Whatever. Just come help me." He trotted back to his room.

Norah heaved a sigh to the ceiling.

The faux fur hat was so soft in her hands. She brought it to her nose and could almost smell the baked goods of the quaint Austrian town again.

7

"She's afraid of fire," Frost said as he stomped through the condo's entry way and into the open kitchen.

Leaf spoon-tasted a pot of stew, which he busied stirring on the stove. "Wait, who are we talking about? Your face looks like a sour lemon in a kimchi bath."

"That human girl." Frost waved his arm impatiently. "Norah."

"Ooh, the one you want to use for your selfish scheme?"

Frost threw a snowball at his shoulder. "Don't put it like that." He stormed over to a chair at the table. Ice crystals began inching up the flower vase from where his elbow perched.

"Ah-ah, no freezing the flowers!" Leaf pointed with the spoon. "Or I'll not share this delicious beef stew with you."

The ice backtracked.

"So what if she's afraid? What's a little fear of fire? It can be scary at times, you know. Believe me, I've seen enough forest fires," said Leaf.

The green vine above the kitchen sink and window turned maroon.

"Fires are a part of winter! People need to cook and bake and keep warm. It's something she'll encounter every day with this job," Frost ranted.

The vine shifted back to green.

"Perhaps she's more suited to summer than winter," mused Leaf.

Frost flung an icicle dart. "Don't even think about stealing away my ticket to freedom. She came to *me*, not you," he growled.

Leaf waved his palms and leaned to the side as the icicle sailed past. "I was only suggesting."

The vine tinted red.

"*Ah-ah*, we agreed the kitchen would be my domain!" Leaf shook a finger at him.

The green returned.

"Fine." Frost sulked over to the living room space. The potted plants there became encrusted in a layer of snow and ice while he lounged on the sofa.

Leaf gave a theatrical shudder. "Winter is so vicious…"

The next evening, Frost walked along the length of powerlines in Concord, as easily as if he were strolling down a street, his hands in his coat pockets, until he reached the drafty window of the old house and its flaking painted sides.

He bent down and tapped his knuckles against the glass, then watched without any emotion as the human girl inside hurried to put her shoes and coat on.

She opened the window, her smile beaming up at him full of eagerness. A small part of him wondered why she was so eager. She had a home, a family, everything he could ever want. And yet, she always seemed glad to get away from it all.

"Hi, Frost!"

He held out his hand and lifted her up to stand on his shoes. "Good evening, Norah. Care to go for a stroll?"

She leaned back nervously, trying not to let her face get too close to his as she held onto him. "You bet! What foreign place are we visiting, this time?" she asked, tucking hair behind her ear.

"To the foreign place of Boston." He winked. "And I doubt you've ever seen it the way we will tonight."

He took off, silencing her beginning question, and bits of ice like glitter streamed behind them as they flew southward, past Concord and over the highways. At his magical speed, it wasn't long before the city's bright lights and skyscrapers emerged above the dark horizon.

He shifted Norah so that she was beside him, his arm holding her waist, so she could stretch out her arms. "Whoa, I feel like a bird!" she exclaimed, completely enthralled, her arms out like wings.

They soared over expensive hotel rooftops, and along the icy docks, and then weaved between the towering buildings and the tall Custom House Tower and its old clock face. Everywhere they looked, Christmas lights shone brightly and streets were alive with people. Frost angled their flight lower.

"Won't people see us?" Norah asked worriedly above the blare of Christmas music and chatter.

"I use glamour, remember?" He smirked back at her.

The Boston Common came into view and its grand Christmas tree glowed like a beacon, brought there from Nova Scotia. "It's tradition," Frost told her, "as thanks for Boston's vital aid after the Halifax Explosion—a terrible disaster where two ships collided, one carrying high explosives, and the result left almost two-thousand people dead. Boston was quick to send help and supplies, and those in Nova Scotia have never forgotten it."

Norah stared at the tree, which glittered tonight like a bejeweled monolith.

They dropped down to an ice-skating pond, and Frost's shoes slid along as if he were wearing ice skates. He held Norah's hands, pulling her along with him around the pond.

Children laughed and chased their friends across the ice, and a man teased his girlfriend when she kept falling over.

Norah's hazel eyes were alight, almost as bright as the decorated tree.

"You have a child-like sense of wonder," Frost observed. "That's good. Winter is all about tricks and fun."

"What tricks?" she asked him.

Frost strummed the lyre inside his coat, and a chilly gust wended its way over the pond, shoving people's legs out from under them. They tumbled and slid with a chorus of grunts and surprised exclamations.

"Hey, that's a mean trick. Someone could get hurt," she reprimanded him, tipping her head back.

"Then what would *you* do?" Frost pulled out the lyre, placing it in her hands, and let her go so that she skated backwards on her own.

She struggled to keep her balance and gripped the lyre tightly.

"Remember: imagine what you want to have happen."

He watched as she tried to steady her gaze and her legs, and she plucked two high notes with care—probably fearing a repeat of last time.

A light gust carried a cloud of glittering ice dust around the pond. It weaved around the children playfully and twirled above their heads before heading up into the sky, leaving the kids to gaze after it wonderingly. The glittering dust vanished into the silver clouds and moon beyond the buildings.

Norah turned to him for approval, face beaming, her simple brown hair framing her soft cheekbones.

Frost cocked his head and shrugged his shoulders. "Not bad, I guess."

Her lips formed a mock pout, which involuntarily made him chuckle. He caught her hand and pulled her back up into the air with him.

People were keeping warm by a small fire burning in a pit, and he lowered to just a few yards away from it. He studied her face, curious to see her reaction. "If you're hands are cold, you can warm them," he told her.

Norah stared at the fire for one tense moment, then turned her face away, trying not to acknowledge its existence.

"Maybe I'll warm myself up a bit." Frost moved towards the small blaze, tugging on her hand. But she resisted, pulling her hand free, and watched as he halted before the orange-yellow glow and smoky crackle. He raised his palms to the heat and cast a quick glance back. Norah had turned her back, patiently waiting, her breath making puffs of mist.

This girl, why couldn't she at least *try* to face her fears? How was he supposed to work with this?

He abandoned his attempt and strode back to her. She cast him a sidelong look, perhaps somewhat suspiciously.

He just grinned and took her elbow, gliding them up several feet above the ground and letting their feet dangle. He flew them toward the docks, where decorated trees and the great trellis made Columbus Park as bright as day. The colors reflected off the nearby lapping waves.

Norah pulled free and landed before the trellis, gazing up in dream-like wonder at the blue and gold Christmas lights that formed a glowing archway along it. She caught Frost's sleeve and tugged him underneath the arch with her.

"The blue lights twinkle like ice faeries, don't they?" she said, skipping underneath the trellis, her face tipped upwards.

"They're sprites, actually."

"Ah, yes. *You're* the real ice faery." Norah spun around on her heels.

"Do you like the winter lyre that much, then?" he asked her.

She turned back, her expression a question, then she looked down at her hand and suddenly remembered the lyre was still in her grip. "Oh...I didn't notice. It felt so normal in my hand," she said. Her tone sounded both surprised and curious.

"It makes a more cheerful sound with you than it does me. Perhaps you are meant to wield it," he said. He sauntered beneath the glowing arch, coming to a halt before her.

"No, no. It's yours," she said, shaking her head, and offered the lyre back. He tucked it into his black wool coat.

"I can't wield the lyre forever. One day, I'll have to step down from being the Winter Guardian, and pass this on to someone else," he said, averting his gaze. "I hope it will go to someone who appreciates it. Someone, perhaps...like you." His eyes met hers then. Hazel really was a pretty eye color.

"Me...?" she said faintly, hand lifting to her chest. "I...no, no." She turned to the side. "I have responsibilities, a brother to take care of, and far too many things to worry about." She turned her head slightly back towards him. "Why would you even ask that? I thought you wanted to spend more time with me, not hire me."

Frost's cold pulse quickened. "Of course, I want to spend

more time with you." He worked to ease her concern. "That's the whole point. If you can learn how to help me with my autumn and winter seasonal work, then we can spend more time together. You would wield the lyre for me. That was all I meant."

She folded her arms together for warmth and turned further towards him. "I can't promise anything. I've got a lot on my plate right now," she said plainly.

Frost crossed the distance between them and looped his arm around her elbow, guiding her out from under the trellis. "I would never add to your burdens, Norah. I promise." The ground shrunk beneath them in flight, and waves soon lapped below their feet.

"Where are we going?" she asked with an undernote of worry, observing the dark waters they flew over.

"I mentioned I had a condo in Boston, didn't I? It's time I invited you over for some hot cocoa." He almost said wine, but he wasn't sure what the legal age limit was nowadays.

She seemed to like the suggestion, though a line of worry remained across her forehead. He carried them across Boston Harbor and dipped down towards the entrance to one of the taller glass buildings located at the waterfront.

He berated himself inwardly. He couldn't afford to let her see how desperate he was that she take over the winter lyre job. He couldn't afford to frighten her away.

Norah followed Frost through the grand glass doors and wide foyer of the ultra-luxury condominium building. Shiny elevators and calming instrumental music lifted them to one of the higher floors.

The elevator doors opened, and a row of chandeliers lit their way across a tiled hallway, over to a glossy black door, which unlocked at Frost's cardkey. He gestured for her to enter first.

It was like stepping inside a modern palace—all those luxurious rooms and wide surfaces you can only see online but never visit in person, unless you were flabbergastingly rich. Windows reaching from floor to ceiling, chandelier light fixtures, a balcony that was more like a deck, with plump sofas, and a glass staircase leading up to a second floor.

She was so overcome by the display of wealth that she wandered right past the open kitchen space and the person standing there, until he spoke.

"Hey, you brought Miss Special over!"

Norah whirled around. She couldn't spot the speaker until he moved away from a curtain of vines growing above the kitchen sink and window. Leaves seemed to be stuck in his clothes and hair, too.

She blinked several times, trying to figure that out, before it became clear that the small leaves were *growing* in his auburn hair. Threads of moss wove up his bare arms and muscle-toned shoulders, and over a tank shirt—similar to how frost patterns and snowflakes decorated Frost. Even the tops of his bare feet had fine fern moss.

If summer and everything vibrant could have a persona, it would be this guy—or woodland faery. His ears were pointed like a faery's.

"Only for a little while," replied Frost.

"Hi there! I'm Jules Leaf," he introduced himself with a bow, hand to chest. He rounded the counter, where he'd been chopping carrots, and lifted her hand lightly in his. Tendrils of moss tickled her skin. "Can I say what a pleasure it is to finally meet you? Frost has been talking about you nonstop! You're all he seems to think about, these days."

Norah swallowed, trying not to show how surprisingly glad that made her feel.

"Don't put ideas in her head, you romance freak," said Frost. "Norah, don't mind him. He's the Summer Guardian, and when you have weird seasons like spring to watch over, it makes you whacky." He fished out two mugs and started a kettle boiling.

"Oh cry me an onion, you've got Halloween in your seasons—and that's as whacky as they come," Leaf fired back over his shoulder. "Not to mention that Valentine's Day is in February…" he added, with a little eyebrow wiggle.

Frost cleared his throat and promptly ignored him.

"You can have a seat in the living room, Norah." Frost indicated with a chin nod the wide space ahead, off to the right, where a wall made entirely of windows showed the Boston harbor and glimmers of distant Christmas lights.

She would have taken her shoes off, but the living room floor looked like chilled ice and the rug crusted white. Thankfully, the sofa was a comfortable temperature when she sat down. Potted plants about the living space were also white, their leaves and flowers frozen over.

"Look at her, she's freezing! I told you the living room should be mine. How can we be hospitable to guests while freezing their toes and noses off?" Leaf complained.

Norah glanced from the living room to the rest of the condo's open room spaces and the floor above. Each space was either decorated in green and warmth or ice and cold.

"Fine, then I'll take the kitchen. As if we ever have guests over, anyway," grumbled Frost, getting out the cocoa powder tin and stirring.

"No! I refuse to eat my food frozen over, as does every other living thing in the world."

Frost let out a huff. "There's no winning with you." He carried the two mugs into the living room and handed one to her shaped like half of a snowman.

She sipped, letting the chocolate heat spread through her

body and the steam warm her nose.

"How have you been?" Frost sat beside her, a small gap between them. "You mentioned that some things in life weren't going so well."

Norah glanced his way, not quite meeting his gaze, her heart thumping. She nodded, not trusting her voice to be steady.

"If you ever need help, you can tell me." His hand pressed lightly over hers against the mug. "Whatever it is you need. Just think of me and call my name, and I'll hear you."

"Or me," Leaf piped in, taking the adjacent sofa chair.

Frost threw him a sharp glare.

Norah made a small laugh to hide her awkward blush. "I'll keep that in mind. Thanks." She took another sip of velvety hot chocolate.

"You seem to have a fascination for faeries," Frost remarked. "Even buying books on the subject."

Norah lifted her shoulders to her ears in a shrug. "Do I have to admit it? Faeries are cool, especially those that can fly. Go on, laugh at me."

Frost tilted his head. "How would you like to become a faery yourself?"

Norah almost snorted out hot chocolate. "*Me?*"

"You could fly, you could travel the world, you could do many things," he said, his words enticing. "If you become the next Winter Guardian, you would be a faery like me. No worries, no burdens, nothing but making sure that autumn and winter stay balanced around the world."

Norah shifted uncomfortably on the sofa. No worries or burdens…*sheesh*, that did sound nice.

"If you want to. It's entirely your choice, Norah. I just want to give you the offer first, before I choose someone else. You could be my apprentice and test the job out for a while, if you like. The winter lyre is happy with you. I can feel its lighter tone, its merry song, when you touch the strings."

Norah glanced over at Leaf, who was working hard to keep his eyes on his glass of wine and nothing else. "I…will think about it," she said, gazing at the chocolaty depths in her mug. "Hey, Frost. You said you used to be human? What was your life like before? How did you end up becoming the Winter Guardian?"

Frost lifted his chin, his midnight eyes locked on the coffee table before them, thumb and index finger pressed to the side of his face. She noticed the brief glance that Leaf cast his way.

"It was the 1880s, when life was quite dull and stuffy," he finally said. "I fell off a ship sailing to Ireland and drowned, but the old Winter Guardian called to me and offered to give me a new life if I would take his place. And so, here I am." He gestured to all of him with a wave.

Norah tried not to look surprised. "That sounds rough… Sorry."

He shrugged, his brow creasing. "Nothing for you to be sorry about."

She swallowed. "Does this mean I have to *die* to get this job?" she asked, trying not to exclaim.

"No, no, I didn't." Leaf waved his palm to ease her worry.

She leaned forward and nodded over to Leaf. "What's your story, then?"

Leaf downed his wine and lounged back. "Ah, it was back in good old 1862 when the old Summer Guardian found and trained me! A blast of fun it was making things grow and bringing hot summer vacations to people. Oh, the stories I could tell you! But I didn't die and get brought back to life, like ol' Frosty here."

She didn't miss the icy look Frost cast his way. Norah's mouth pursed in thought. "Did you miss your families? Or could you still stay with them?"

To that they were both silent. It was Leaf who finally spoke.

"A part of me did miss them. But I didn't age the same as them anymore, see, and so I had to fake my own death. But I was able to watch my siblings grow up, from afar." His gaze clouded over and a dark shadow crossed his features. "That is, until a vicious ice storm caused their vehicle to crash."

His grip on the wine glass made her fear it might break.

Then, he lifted his face and the merriment returned to his clay-colored eyes. "Life has been good, otherwise! Being a Guardian has many perks and fits my whimsical nature. I could picture you as one of us; the lifestyle suits you." He pointed to her with the glass.

"Maybe..." Norah mumbled. It wasn't like she had anybody else to live for but her brother.

Frost set down his mug. "It's late. I should probably get you back to your home."

She nodded vaguely, all the worries of the world creeping back into her mind.

She waved goodbye to Leaf from the balcony of their condo and was suddenly airborne with Frost.

"That was sad about Leaf's family," she said quietly.

Frost agreed absentmindedly. "I don't know the details. The previous Frost was Winter Guardian during that time."

Norah felt a sadness as the elegant glass buildings and cheerful lights were replaced with cramped, run-down houses on a dim, potholed street—back home in Concord. She slipped through her bedroom window with practiced ease, and watched as Frost soared away, the scarf flapping behind him.

Homework sat on her desk, like reality stabbing little knives into her gut, and she found herself longing for the realm of fantasy and faery, where worries could be left behind.

Should she take Frost's offer? Become a faery, live life with Frost by her side?

Like Bilbo, she could go off on a real adventure.

But then, what about Tim? She refused to abandon him, so…could she somehow use this Guardian job to find a better home for him? Was there a solution to their problem hidden somewhere in all of this?

'What should I do? God, please tell me.'

8

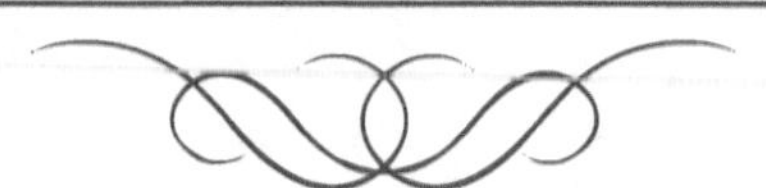

"MOM, WHY AREN'T YOU AT work?" Norah came down for breakfast and saw her mom making waffles and humming a disco tune.

Something must have happened. Rarely did anything ever put their mom in a good mood. Let alone to the point where she was actually making waffles.

Her stomach cringed, afraid to find out the reason.

Tim was at the table, munching cereal and looking just as uneasy, glancing about and tapping his feet together under the table.

"Mom?" she tried again, stepping nearer to the fake-marble counter.

Mom finished spooning batter onto the waffle iron and

tapped the ladle merrily against the bowl before turning to her. "The best thing ever happened late last night!" she said, her voice holding in a squeal of excitement. "I wanted to tell you right away, but I made myself wait until morning." She held up her hand, showing her fingers. "See this? Bob asked me to marry him!"

A diamond ring sparkled like a meteorite coming down to destroy Norah's life. Her soul sank into dread, while her mother's lifted into pure thrill.

Tim's spoon fell loudly into his cereal bowl.

"Marry…him…?" Norah's lips could barely move, dumbfounded as she was.

"Yes! And do you know what that means? We're selling the house! We can finally get out of this rickety, old place and move down to Boston where Bob lives." Mom held her ring-finger to her chest. "It's a luxury condo! Can you imagine? We're rich, Norah! We're moving up in the world! And I'll have a real walk-in closet." This time she did squeal and bounce on her heels. "I'll have shelves for all my name-brand shoes and purses, just like the celebrities do!"

Moving? Moving in with Bob?

Norah suddenly regretted all her complaints about the old house. It wasn't an easy place to live in, but at least it wasn't a nightmare where she had to fear running into Bob around every corner.

"No, Mom. We can't." Norah shook her head vigorously, hair strands slapping her cheeks. "We can't live with Bob."

Mom's happy dance stuttered to a halt.

"He's a bully who doesn't give a crap about us, and for some weird reason, you never seem to realize that." Norah's voice rose.

"Now see here, don't you talk like that about your step-dad." Mom waggled a finger, her smile twisting into a grimace. "I'm still your mother, and you'll do what I say."

Norah backed away, still shaking her head. She caught Tim's shoulder and urged him to his feet. "You can do what you want with your life, Mom. But we have our own lives, too. Our schools are here, my job is here—we can't just up and leave. Besides, you know it would cause you a lot of headaches, too," she pressed. "You don't really want us getting in the way of you and Bob spending time together, so soon, do you? We'll go live with Aunt Karin and finish school, instead."

Mom watched them edge out of the kitchen towards the door, crossing her arms and chewing on her lip.

"The law might consider you an adult now, but *not* Tim. If I say you both come with me, then you're coming with me." Her tone brooked no argument. "But it *is* halfway through the school year, and it'd be a pain to transfer you both..." she mumbled, considering.

"Well, I guess if Karin doesn't mind, you can stay with her until summer. Either way," Mom slapped her hands together, "we've got loads of packing to do! The new buyer is coming next week."

The door swung open to the small room in Aunt Karin's apartment, which Norah and Tim would have to share, a small bed on each side. Norah stood in the doorway, suitcase swaying in her hand.

"I'm sorry I can't offer better," said Karin.

"No, no. I'm just glad you offered at all," said Norah, truly grateful.

Tim pushed past and claimed the left-side bed, heaving his suitcase on top and unzipping it with practiced ease.

Central heating kept the room warm that night, but she missed the clanking hum of the old furnace that had become so familiar. The single window had no drafts, but it didn't have a view of the powerlines that Frost would walk along.

Everything that had felt and smelled of home over the years was now gone, and her mind struggled to comprehend it.

How was she going to find a second job, and save up money, when they had an hour-long commute to Concord? What were she and Tim going to do when the school year ended and Mom came for them? She was old enough to live on her own, but she couldn't leave Tim alone to suffer through that.

"Whatever it is you need. Just think of me and call my name, and I'll hear you."

Norah quietly lifted the window open. Cold air swept her hair back, and she leaned her head forward. A streetlamp cast shadows in the alley below, and above, the moon struggled to glow through sheaves of thick haze.

"Frost," she whispered to the air, putting all thought into the shape of his face, his midnight eyes and dark eyelashes. As if picturing the pale Guardian could somehow summon him.

A frigid gust made her choke and draw back, pelting her with ice dust.

Then a shadow moved towards the window, snowflakes shimmering in the figure's black hair. Frost held out his hands for her.

It had worked! Grinning, and trying to be quiet, she crawled over the sill and into his waiting arms.

"Well, you're in quite a predicament," said Frost, after she had explained her situation and distress. They walked through Boston's Quincy Market, strands of white lights bejeweling the rows of trees like fireflies. The place was alive with Christmas festivities, bright shops, and freezing vendors.

"Don't remind me," she grumbled, her breath making clouds.

"Does this mean you'll take my offer?"

She frowned up at him. "Happy, are you? I'm miserable, and you want to use it for your own benefit."

He shrugged. "It's your loss if you reject this. Not mine."

She looked sidelong up at him again. It was hard to read his expression, what he might be thinking. But there was still that bit of emptiness, a lonely hint behind his frost-rimmed irises. "Maybe I could give it a try, for a while. Be your apprentice, like you suggested."

Was that a spark of hope that just flashed across Frost's features?

"But I can't abandon my brother, like you and Leaf did your families," she added firmly. "If I become the Winter Guardian, even if I can't be with Tim in the same way anymore, I want to at least find him a good home."

Frost's lips pursed for a moment, as if he might argue, but then he nodded. "Excellent. Let's begin with the basics." His arm snaked around her waist and pulled her with him into the sky.

They touched down on a low rooftop building overlooking the market. His swift hand pulled out the winter lyre and pressed it into her palms. The ice runes in the wood glowed as if alive.

"The lyre is sensitive to emotion," he told her. "As you play the strings, your emotions can determine how strong the wind blows, or how wild it snows. I'm sure you've noticed: cheerful feelings create delicate effects, while negative feelings can create a storm."

She lifted her head. "And when you're sad?"

He paused and averted his gaze. "It rains ice or sleet."

"Like tears," she said quietly. Her fingers traced the ice-smooth strings. "I should probably be in the right frame of mind before I play this. I've got enough anger to fuel a hurricane, right now."

Frost cracked an unexpected laugh, seeming to surprise even himself. He then tried to mask it by giving her a sideways smile. "With practice, you'll learn to suppress your emotions."

Sitting down, she held the lyre in her lap and watched as patches of fog shifted between the streets and skyscrapers. "I wouldn't suppress them—that'd be nothing but a disaster waiting to happen. I'd try to redirect them into more positive thoughts and emotions, instead... Or so a well-known psychologist once said."

Frost cocked his head in thought, brow furrowed.

After making such a statement, she felt the need to prove her point, and lifted the small lyre. The wood arm rested against her chest, and she imagined a light carpet of frost in her mind. Then she followed the lyre's draw, letting it guide her fingers to four notes, creating an undulating, light rhythm. She thought of winter, the beauty of sparkling ice in moonlight, and her emotions filled with a pleasant calm, pouring into the melody.

"Norah..."

She paused and opened her eyes at his quiet call, at first worried that she'd created a disaster.

The marketplace below them was shimmering a silvery white, and people stopped in their tracks to marvel all around them. Frost covered the ground, the stones, the trees, in long trailing feather patterns, detailed and vivid as if painted by a whimsical artist.

Norah grinned and glanced over at Frost's dangling jaw before he quickly shut it. He cleared his throat and looked elsewhere. "I don't think you'll be needing much teaching, at this rate," he muttered. "It took me years to figure that trick out..."

She gave a small giggle. She'd never been a natural at anything before, other than at drawing.

"Ooh, cider doughnuts!" She pointed at a cart and urged Frost to get up.

They floated off the roof and, moments later, were strolling along the frosted pavement and chewing soft, hot cider doughnuts. She savored the cinnamon and apple flavors.

"So, I know about Leaf," she started a conversation. "But what about you? Do you miss your family? Do you have any relatives?"

Frost's black shoes began to crunch the ice with every step, as if weighted down by something invisible. He turned his chin away. "They grew old and died, forgetting all about me. But they lived a good life, I think." He brushed a finger across his nose. "I missed them at first, but…after one-hundred-and-forty years, the feeling wore off."

She eyed him sidelong. "I find it hard to believe they would forget you."

He was silent for a moment. "Well, maybe it's just easier for me to believe that."

She stuffed the rest of the doughnut into her mouth, blinking at him. She wanted to ask again if he had any relatives—like descendants of siblings—but judging by that answer, he'd probably never bothered to search for them. "Do you have any other faery friends to keep you company? Is there a realm of the Fae up in Ireland, like the legends say?"

He smirked. "You really like fairy tales, don't you? But why should I tell you anything more about me, when you won't even tell me why you're afraid of fire?"

Norah's mouth twisted to the side. He knew how to hit a soft spot.

She wanted to say something bratty and tell him off, but his hand wrapped around hers as they walked, fingers entwining, his thumb stroking the back of her hand.

A giddy shiver ran through her. She lifted her gaze. His expression spoke of care and longing—a longing that only she could fill. Or was that what he wanted her to think?

"When I was eight, I started a fire by accident in our house," she found herself suddenly telling him. "I was playing with a scented candle, but then I got distracted and left it alone on a windowsill. Fire caught on the curtains…" She blinked as the memory of smoke and heat and crying resurfaced.

"Mom ran outside with baby Tim, but me and Dad were trapped on the second floor. He threw me out the window to Mom. But…" A sob tried to strangle her words in her throat. "He couldn't fit through the window himself. He was overweight, and I remember screaming and crying for him to jump out, not understanding… The smoke suffocated him before the firemen arrived. He died, and it was all my fault."

There. She'd finally let the words spill out, her guilt pooling like ink around her miserable form.

She coughed and wiped her cheeks. "Fire reminds me of that day. And… I just hope the saying is true, that time heals all wounds, or something like that."

Frost stared at the ground ahead of his shoes, his smile gone. His thumb caressed over her knuckles one by one. "I still miss them," he said suddenly, his voice quiet. "When the night is at its darkest, and I long for home."

They halted before one of the firefly-lit trees, and his shoulder pressed against hers. "You have to let go of the guilt you've been carrying all these years, Norah. You keep a cheerful face, but it will never be fully real until you do." He turned to face her, narrowing the gap between them, and brought his free hand to brush the hair back from her cheek. The firefly lights made the snowflakes in his hair glitter.

"How am I supposed to do that?" she struggled to say. She sucked in her lips.

Four fingers brushed down her cheek, following one of her tears. "The Creator of this world knows each of our paths, where our lives will go, and where they are meant to end. I don't claim to have any answers, but perhaps your father was being spared from something painful that would happen later on—something he wouldn't have been able to bear."

She paused to consider his words.

Mom. When Norah thought of her, she wasn't exactly the loyal type of wife. Would she have run around on Dad, and had them all suffer through a divorce? She knew Dad's kind heart could never have survived a betrayal like that.

Maybe some things happened for reasons that Norah didn't want to consider…

She squeezed Frost's hand and looked into his eyes. "Thank you," she whispered. And she wasn't sure if she was leaning towards him, or him towards her, but their noses were suddenly close, and she could feel his light-feather breath. "If I do become a faery like you, you'll stay by my side, won't you? You'll take me to meet lots of other faeries, and we'll live out our long lives together?"

The corners of Frost's lips twitched downward slightly. "Of course." He pulled back, the possibility of a kiss now lost.

His back went stiff as he steered her around the firefly trees. "It's late. Let me take you home."

9

NORAH COULDN'T FALL ASLEEP WITHOUT the hum and white noise of her old room's electric fan. So, perching a drawing pad on her lap, she made a sketch of Frost: It portrayed his slightly tousled dark hair, dusted with snowflakes, and his scarf flapping in the wind, all outlined in charcoal. She added the mischievous curve of his lips and the pointed tip of his nose.

But his eyes…the emotion was hard to pinpoint. They kept staring back at her from the paper, forlorn and empty, as if holding onto a wish that could never be fulfilled.

She let the pencil drop on the bed and analyzed the sketch under her moon-shaped nightlight, trying to be quiet while Tim slept in the bed across from her.

What was it that Frost wished for? It didn't feel as simple as missing his family, but something darker, something she couldn't quite put a name to…

Frost contemplated the advice he'd given Norah. It was easy to give advice to others, but was he learning from any of it himself? It hadn't really occurred to him until now.

The Creator knew their paths, including Frost's, and that drowning in the ocean wouldn't be the end for him. Frost had been brought to the cave of the Winter Dome, at just the right time, to become the next Winter Guardian.

He shook his head. None of it mattered, now. He had served his purpose, carried out his job, for long enough. And with the arrival of Norah, the perfect candidate to take his place, it was surely a sign for him to pass on the Guardian role. He couldn't be wrong about that. It's what he wanted. And yet, why did a small part of him ache?

Frost rounded the glass staircase, headed up towards his room, when Leaf suddenly appeared and stood in his way, arms crossed and leaning back with a disapproving frown.

"What?" Frost moved to go around him.

"You lied to her," said Leaf. "You acted like the two of you would still be together after she takes your place as Guardian."

Frost halted on the stair. "You were *spying* on us?" He said it as if the other matter meant nothing.

Leaf shifted his posture, his tone becoming bitter. "Tell her the truth. Don't feed her false hopes of love and faery friends when there's nothing."

Frost shrugged. "I don't know if there is nothing. Maybe there are all sorts of faeries lurking about? It's not our job to keep track of them and their realm."

"You're going to die. Doesn't she have a right to know that before she completely throws her heart at you?"

Frost curled his fingers. "Her feelings for me are the only reason she's open to taking the job. So, unless you want to be stuck with me forever, don't interfere!" He marched upstairs past him, shoes clicking the glass. Leaf stared after him.

Inside his wide bedroom of icicles and dangling snowflakes, Frost shrugged out of his coat and unwound the black scarf. He could still feel the warmth of her cheek beneath his fingers, the smoothness of her brown hair. When she smiled, the dent in her lower lip stretched out.

Why had he encouraged her to like him? He ran his hands through his hair, feeling agitated.

He wasn't out to break hearts. He'd never been that type of person before. And yet…

"You'll stay by my side, won't you? You'll take me to meet lots of other faeries, and we'll live out our long lives together?"

Together… If only that were possible.

What would together feel like? To shepherd the seasons with someone at his side? To share this life?

"…Doesn't matter," he mumbled to himself, balling up the scarf. "It can never happen."

The choices were either die now, or go on living in solitude.

And he knew which one he had already chosen.

Sleet pattered against the car windows the next morning, as Norah drove herself and Tim to Concord for school. She leaned forward, snatching a glance at the dark underbellies of the clouds overhead and their swirly, puffy patterns.

Was Frost upset about something? Were his emotions making this weather?

The school hours that day passed without much incident,

except for the typical teenage drama. She laid low, and when it came time, she hurried off to pick up Tim, shivering against the cold rain, the ice melting to liquid under her boots.

"Sorry you have to stay here and wait," she told Tim as they hurried into The Fast Noodle for her work shift. She sat him at a table at the far back. "Aunt Karin will come pick you up in an hour."

Tim yanked off his wet coat and gloves and plopped his backpack on the booth bench. "Anything is better than being at Bob's." He made a funny yet grossed-out face. "I've got homework to finish, anyway."

Norah ruffled his hair. "You're a good kiddo."

He batted her hand away, muffling his grin.

Norah donned the red Fast Noodle cap before Manager Jeff could say anything. She stirred fried rice around a large pan and waited for orders—which, on a yucky day like today, were few.

"Few orders today. This weather bad for business!" Jeff motioned skyward, as if something could be done about it.

"It's bad for my cold, too." Freddie sniffled inside a facemask, stirring some now-soggy noodles. He sneezed.

"No sneeze on noodles!" Jeff shouted back, shaking a finger.

"That's what the facemask is for!" Freddie pointed to his nose exasperatedly.

The heavy glass door opened and closed suddenly, and Norah leaned over the counter to see the customer: a young woman with long, green hair.

"Hi, Selk!"

She had on a silvery wetsuit this time under a long, furry coat.

"Norah." Selk met her at the counter. There was a strange amount of water dripping down her hair and clothes and puddling the floor tiles.

Had this crazy girl just gone for a swim? In *this* weather?

"Is there any chance for fast food noodles?" she asked.

"Sure, choose a seat." When Norah brought a ramen bowl over to Selk by the window, water was still dripping down the girl's legs.

"You're soaked," she commented.

Several booths away, Tim pretended to be oblivious while doing homework on an old laptop, but she could tell he was striving to hear every word.

Selk twirled the fork in the noodles, working to slurp them up. "Yes, the river water was nicely cold today," she replied, as if discussing fine weather.

Norah cocked her head to the side. "Are you by any chance not…" her gaze trailed up from the girl's bare feet to the top of her seaweed-colored hair, and she leaned closer to whisper, "…entirely human?"

"Oh." Selk's overly large eyes blinked once. "What gave me away?"

Norah's mouth quirked. Now that Selk had practically admitted to it, Norah felt stupid for not realizing sooner. Selk's strange way of speaking, the wetsuit and swimming in frigid temperatures… But to be fair, there *were* crazy people along the coast who enjoyed going scuba diving during the winter. And maybe her brain had just been too preoccupied with other things.

"What brought you to New England? Are you some kind of mermaid?" She spoke quietly, not letting Tim eavesdrop. He peeked at them over his laptop.

"In a way, yes. I'm a selkie, come from the far northern shores of ice," she answered. "My clan is in dire need. Our frozen home is melting away, and I must find the Guardians of the Seasons."

"Guardians? Do you mean the Season Guardians?" she asked in surprise.

Selk's large eyes lit up. "Yes! You know them?"

Norah nodded.

Selk tapped her hands together joyfully, a bit of webbing between each finger now showing. "I was hoping you would be able to help me—you saw me in the waters when no one else could. My journey will finally be a success."

Norah hushed her. Tim's eyebrows had sailed to the ceiling.

Thankfully, just then, Aunt Karin's car pulled up to the curb to pick him up.

She ushered Tim outside. "I'll be home late, so don't worry," she told him and Karin, and waved as they drove through the next surge of rain.

Home—it felt strange to say that word.

"Can you wait here until my shift is over?" she asked Selk, who then nodded in what was more like a bow. Norah glanced about quickly, hoping no one was watching.

Later, she and Selk stood outside under the restaurant's awning, and Norah called out Frost's name and willed him to come.

He came, rain rolling off his hair and collared coat without dampening a single inch of him. That must be a useful trick.

"Calling for me two days in a row. Is this a good sign, or should I be worried?" he asked, hands in pockets. He regarded the strange girl standing beside her.

"We need a place to talk," Norah said. "Call Leaf, too. Apparently, there's a selkie crisis going on."

The most secure place to talk was, of course, the Guardians' luxury condo in Boston.

Norah watched Selk's amazed reaction, imitating her own back when she first saw the place. Though, to Selk, anything on land was probably fascinating; she wouldn't be able to recognize the splendor of wealth.

Leaf tossed blankets onto the sofa to warm them against the living room's ice décor. He took the chair to the right while Frost took the left.

From the moment Selk met the Summer Guardian, she hadn't been able to take her eyes off of him. To be fair, he was as equally wondrous to look at as Frost, the embodiment of life and vitality and warmth.

"My clan makes their dwellings in the ice along the far north coast," Selk began her story. "In Summer, the ice retreats a bit, and we move into the coastal caves. But…the summer melt has never lasted this long before." She shook her seaweed-green hair. "We do not have the protection of the ice to keep predators at bay, and much of our food has moved off into deeper waters where it is not safe for us to follow. We will starve if things do not change, if the cold season does not return to how it once was." She lifted her head, looking to Frost, then to Leaf. "You are the Season Guardians. Please, you can make winter back to the way it was, can you not?"

Frost had his arms crossed and a leg over one knee. He shared a look with Leaf. "You must be from the Canadian coastline, then," said Frost. "Unfortunately, Selk, I have orders not to interfere with the way of things. The earth is gradually warming due to several factors—and I can't do anything about those factors."

The hope in Selk's face wilted and her chin lowered, damp green waves of hair framing her pale cheekbones and green eyelashes.

"Don't go getting all gloom-and-doom just yet, though, missy!" Leaf hopped to his feet, the little vine leaves in his hair curling and rustling about. "I can help your clan to prepare— help them adapt to warmer waters, and show them alternate food sources. I can't alter the climate for you, but I *can* alter your lifestyle. I'm sure the mermaid pods will be friendly enough to help you out, as well!"

Selk's head lifted, and she focused on Leaf with that same wondrous expression. "Any help will be gratefully accepted. Thank you, Summer Guardian."

"Oh, just call me Leaf." He scratched the back of his auburn head, cheeks flushed. "I'll have your clan adapted to warmer waters in no time, don't you worry! And you may find that you enjoy the change and can do without frigid ol' winter." He winked.

She looked baffled but bowed her head. "I am grateful."

Frost rolled his eyes.

Norah rose from the plush sofa, ice crystals in the rug crunching underfoot. "I should get home, before Tim starts to worry where I am."

Selk moved to stand, when her legs suddenly wobbled.

"See you later, Norah. And *you*," Leaf caught Selk by the shoulder, "are clearly in need of a replenishing soak. We don't want you to become a dried anchovy! At dawn, I'll head out with you to your clan." He lifted Selk in his arms, carrying her through the open rooms to wherever the bathtub was.

"I wish you well, Norah!" Selk said, her legs starting to fuse together into a silvery-gray tail.

"I wish you well, too, Selk! I hope we cross paths again." Norah waved.

10

THE UGLY, LEATHERY CREATURE TASTED the air with its tongue, tasting the smell of hate, as it traveled along the upper winds like burning sulfur.

The scent filled the creature and gave new strength to its many limbs and wings.

It took flight, its mouth open and sucking in the strong emotion like an energizing drink.

Behind and around the creature the winds grew wilder, fiercer. Clouds coalesced and turned in a slow rotation, growing and thickening…

A week passed by. Christmas day was drawing nearer, and Norah's lessons with the winter lyre continued. She made icicles drip down the eaves of buildings and managed to make an ice castle wall rise from the frozen ground.

Frost watched with a satisfied smile, the empty longing behind his eyes less forlorn and more eager now, as if he were anticipating something.

But anticipating what?

She liked to think that he had the same growing feelings for her that she had for him, but she wasn't going to let herself assume that just yet.

"Excellent, Norah. The lake is frozen solid!" Frost hopped from foot to foot, testing the thick layers of ice, not a crack in sight.

"The kids will love skating on it," she said, imagining them all bundled in thick coats and scarves and shuffling about on the ice. "Hey, we should dust some more snow on the ski slopes! December should have more snow than this."

Frost rolled his neck, stretching his muscles. "The earth slowly changes, and the seasons must shift with it. There will be plenty of snow in March."

Norah made a face. "Ugh. I don't want spring to be all muddy and late again."

Frost's back went rigid. Chin raised, he stared ahead, every inch of his posture tensing.

"Frost?" She glanced about, tugging her scarf tighter. But there was nothing she could see as the cause.

"This shouldn't be," he spoke suddenly, gaze latched onto something unseen.

"What?" she asked in a hushed tone.

Frost snatched the winter lyre from her and shot up into the sky.

"Hey, wait!" she cried out, her hand reaching up.

But he was gone, vanishing through a swirling snow vortex.

Norah drew her arms in and shivered, suddenly cold and alone beside a frozen lake far from Portsmouth.

Should she wait? Hah, as if she had a choice.

Dusting off a large boulder, she sat and balled herself up, breathing on her knees for warmth. She almost fell asleep by the time Frost reappeared. Any hint of his previous smile was gone.

"You left me! I could've frozen to death out here! What's going on?" she grouched at him.

Frost hoisted her up in his arms, his brow shadowed and creased with a grimace. "A nor'easter has appeared out of nowhere, heading up the eastern coast," he told her.

"Well, big storms happen sometimes. They're a pain to deal with, but aren't *you* the one who makes them?" she asked, letting herself feel comfortable in his arms, leaning her head against his chest.

Was it her, or did he just flinch at her touch?

"That's the problem—I *didn't* make it."

"Maybe your emotions did? Like when it rains ice pellets?"

"No, that would affect *this* region, not North Carolina. This is a bigger problem, and one I can't solve on my own." He took flight, curving southward, the frozen lake below shrinking away.

"Then I'll help!" she offered eagerly.

He glanced down at her, some warmth returning to his features. "You're not a full-fledged Guardian yet. There's nothing you can do against a weather demon."

The steep rooftops of the coastal city approached them. "A *what*? There's such a thing like that?"

"We Guardians have to be mindful and careful. A weather demon will take any advantage it can to disrupt our work and create chaos," he explained. "I don't know what has given this one so much fuel that it could create a near-hurricane, and in just one day."

He let her down into her bedroom window. She slipped her legs through but turned her torso back toward him. "Will you be safe?" She gazed up into his midnight eyes rimmed in feathery ice.

He flashed her a smirk. "I won't be destroyed so easily. But you stay indoors—don't any of you venture outside for anything, until the weather clears."

Selk sat upon the rocky shore, where ice and snow had once kissed the arctic waters, her gray seal tail half submerged in the calm saltwater.

From the caves nearby, her people filed out into the ocean. She watched as Leaf hovered in the air above a patch of pale green water he had formed: a patch of warm water for the selkies to swim in and out of, and get their bodies accustomed to warmer temperatures. It had taken a week for the warmth to not feel like a shock to their silky pelts.

Leaf glided over to the rocks and landed beside her, the green moss and leaves making him stand out vividly upon the barren landscape. How strange it was to see him again, and so clearly—more than just the fuzzy memory she had from childhood, long ago when she'd peeked above the ocean surface and seen him melt ice away to reveal rocky crags for the sea birds to nest upon.

"I think they'll be ready to travel soon. There's a wide bay in southern Canada that should sustain the clan, for now," Leaf told her.

Selk's mind returned to the present. "Good news that is," she replied, casting him a shy smile, tucking green hair behind her fin-like ears, which she'd kept hidden before now.

"How did you know to find me?" Leaf regarded her with a deep curiosity. "Not many people, human or otherwise, believe in the Season Guardians' existence."

Her gaze flickered furtively to him, and her tail flapped the water like someone nervous might tap their foot. "I saw you once before, when I was a young pup. You flew over the waters of the shore and made the seaweed beneath thrive. I watched as you cleared away space for the seabirds on the rocks, melting the ice back. You matched the description of one of our people's ancient myths, and I was fascinated… Ah, it is embarrassing." She lowered her face so that her green hair hid her expression and trailed down her pale shoulders to the gray seal-like pelt that covered her chest and lower half.

"Spying on me without me knowing?" Leaf's tone was amused. "Well, you must be quite a skilled ocean hunter if you could pull that off. I doubt many fish get away from you."

She couldn't help the grin that grew.

"How is it you remain the same as back then?" She reached to lightly touch his cheek. "Young face, barely a wrinkle or change that I can tell, even after so many years?"

"I do age, just very slowly." He leaned in as if it were a secret. "Until I find the person who's meant to take my place."

"Oh? What happens then?"

"Nothing much. I pass on from this life and into Heaven." He let himself fall back and sprawl atop the rocks, which warmed at his touch.

"You die?" Her large eyes blinked.

"Yes, when the time is right. There can only be one Summer and Winter Guardian at a time, each passing on their power to the next generation—or whatever you want to call it." He observed the deep arctic blue sky overhead.

"That won't be for a long while yet for me, though. There's something I must do before then…" He trailed off into silence.

Selk wanted to inquire about what he meant, but a vortex of snow opened up in the sky, and Frost came sailing through.

"Frost? What the heck, you can't be here yet! Give the selkies more time to prepare before you go fooling around with the weather. I'm taking them south to a bay," Leaf began to gripe, sitting upright, a glint of anger behind his clay-colored gaze.

Frost landed, icing the rock that his shoes touched upon. "It's *you* who's been fooling around with the weather," he snapped. "The Nymph of Seasons always warns us never to let our anger build up, or else that anger will become fuel for weather demons."

"What are you going on about?" Leaf rose and crossed his arms in a show of exasperation.

"Have you not sensed it? A nor'easter is headed up the coastline, and it wasn't *my* doing!"

Leaf took a moment to register what he was saying. "A weather demon? Such a strong one? But we've been careful. I mean, we dislike each other and all, but we don't let hatred fester inside us. Where did it get such fuel? It can't have been from me." He touched his chest. "You've been rather callous and glum lately, though. Are you sure it isn't feeding off of *you*?"

Frost opened his mouth, then stopped what he was about to say.

Leaf was the more cheerful of the two of them. He had no reason that Frost could think of to be harboring hate or malice, did he?

While Frost, on the other hand, had been nothing but miserable, eager to be rid of his Guardian work and leave this world.

Perhaps it was because of Frost himself, after all.

"I can't fight it alone," he finally admitted.

After a moment, Leaf nodded and held out his fist. "Let's go kick some weather demon butt."

11

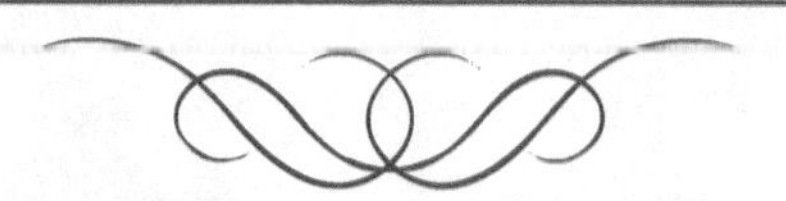

FROST SAILED HIGH IN THE ATMOSPHERE, and Leaf materialized near him in a swirl of leaves. Below them was the long eastern coastline of North America, and there, swirling like a massive whirlpool of cloud, was the cyclone, now riding over New Jersey and cloaking a great swath of landmass beneath its churning fury.

But it was what hovered deep within the cyclone's calm eye that held Frost's attention. He readied his fingers along the winter lyre.

"Ready, Snowflake?" said Leaf with an eager glint.

"More than you are, Weedling."

In unison they dove, descending through the layers of moist atmosphere. Down to the cyclone. Down into the dark, calm eye at its center.

The cacophony of roaring wind from the walls of cloud all around them grew, yet no wind touched them within the eye of the storm, and no precipitation fell. The walls of the cyclone rose to block the sun from their view.

And there the creature was: hovering in the storm's center, with its twisted leathery wings outspread. The weather demon hissed when it saw them descending toward it.

Frost strummed three strong notes on the lyre, and Leaf whistled a shrill note through his summer flute.

Icicles like knives rained down, and hot lightning forked towards the demon.

It dodged the lightning easily but had to use an arm to block one of the icicles, which stabbed through and took its arm clean off.

The demon screamed angrily, revealing its many other arms and wings, and shot up through the air at them.

Frost swerved out of the way of a handful of claws reaching to rip him open.

The demon careened into Leaf, even as he summoned vines from his body to whip the creature. It reeled back angrily, and Frost spotted blood on Leaf's shoulder.

Frost ran his hands along the lyre, weaving a thundering tune, summoning hailstones.

Balls of ice came hurtling from the walls of cloud at his call, and they circled him like little planets as he advanced toward the demon.

The demon flashed out its claws. But its arms couldn't reach past the circle of hailstones spinning around Frost, which pummeled and injured its twisted hands. With a flap of its leathery wings, it flew up and then curved around, firing from its back a volley of spines dripping green venom at them.

Frost shielded against the attack with a thick slab of ice,

and Leaf wrapped himself in thick tree bark.

The spines bounced away.

Leaf flung out vines, which snaked through the air, catching and wrapping around one of the demon's wings and several limbs.

More venomous spines fired out. Bark chunks deflected some, and Frost's hailstones crushed others. "Fry it!" he shouted at Leaf.

The flute whistled, and a brilliant flash of white tore through the air towards the entangled weather demon.

The nor'easter hit Portsmouth, and the wind howled beyond the apartment's windows like a living beast. The streetlamps highlighted a whirling blizzard of white while Norah and Tim watched the big storm through the glass, the electricity struggling to stay on as it flickered, and Aunt Karin hurried to fill water jugs and cook up meals.

Whenever the power went out during winter in New Hampshire, it was a huge pain in the backside. Unless you could afford a whole-house generator, that is. Which, of course, her family never could. She hoped that being in an apartment, now, would mean better electricity service.

Norah kept her sights beyond the windowpane, trying to see if Frost was up there somewhere engaged in battle.

She curled her feet underneath her and flipped through the pages of the faery artwork book. Her finger traced along a blue rain faery, whose hair and skin were translucent as water.

What strange creatures would she meet once she became a Guardian? Frost kept so silent about it. The allure of possibilities promised an escape from all the turmoil of this dark world.

But whatever happened, Tim was her top priority. She wouldn't up and leave him—not until he was old enough to care for himself. And even then, she couldn't just vanish from his life.

She glanced over at Tim.

He caught her eye and shifted in his seat, still wanting to watch the storm that had been wreaking havoc up the coastline. "Norah," he said quietly, even though Karin wouldn't have been able to hear him with all the bustling noise she was making. "Who was that weird lady at The Fast Noodle? Her hair was green—like real green, not dyed. And who goes walking around wearing a wetsuit?"

Norah flipped a page, offered him a shrug and a little smile. "There are all kinds of people in the world. It's best not to judge." She tried to sound grown up and wise when she said it.

Tim made a disbelieving sound through his nose. "That wasn't a human person. More like a sea witch, or some strange faery creature in one of your books."

Norah looked from the book to Tim. Should she tell him? Would now be the right time?

The lamps in the room suddenly flickered and went out.

"Oh, for pity's sake!" she heard Karin groan to the ceiling. Tim launched to his feet to go find the candles and flashlights, while Norah let her head roll back in dread. No power meant no heating, and they wouldn't be able to flush the toilet or shower.

"Only use the bathroom out of absolute desperation!" Karin called out.

Tim flailed his arms in the air, as if the darkness was drowning him.

After a long day of snow and freezing wind, the storm finally weakened. But not before dumping twenty-five inches of snow or more in some regions, and bringing down power for more than three hundred thousand homes and businesses. For a small state like New Hampshire, it was a big deal. The news said it could have been a lot worse, but thankfully the nor'easter's fuel had run out faster than predicted.

"Thank you, Frost, Leaf," Norah whispered to the sky.

School and work were put on hold until enough of the snow could be plowed off the streets. And the apartment's electricity didn't come back on for three days. Needless to say, during that time, they practically lived at the nearest café which had a working generator.

The nights were frigid, huddled in bed under blankets without any central heating or electric heaters, the air chilling Norah's teeth and lungs and keeping her awake. On the second night, a light tap on the window made her sit up. A shadow hovered there, bits of frost glistening under pale moonlight.

"Frost, you're all right!" she said, leaning out the window.

His expression proudly claimed there could be no other result. "You're managing to survive, I see," he said, peering through the glass at their beds layered with heaps of blankets.

She grunted frustratedly. "Just barely. What I wouldn't give for a shower!"

He smirked. "In that case, how about you come over for a visit?" He held out his arms.

Something rustled off to her left. She didn't have a chance to turn or warn Frost before Tim tumbled out of bed and stuck his head out the window.

"Tim!" she gasped.

Tim blinked against the cold, then shut the window, shivering. "What the heck're you doing, letting more cold air in?" he griped.

Baffled at first, Norah recalled then that she was the only human able to see Frost when he was using glamour.

"Talking to the wind," he muttered. "Do that on your own time." Tim crawled back into his bed, pulling an elf hat down over his head.

Norah stood there, the floor's cold seeping through her socks, and waited until she was sure Tim had dozed off. She carefully opened the window again and climbed onto the sill, sliding the pane back down behind her.

Frost caught her and held her close against him. She held onto his waist as they flew, realizing how much she'd missed this, even though it hadn't been that long.

"Did you kill the weather demon? Did you find out how it was able to make that nor'easter?" she inquired.

"Curious, always so curious," Frost muttered in mock irritation. His lips curled upwards. "We got rid of the creature, if you must know, but we couldn't find whatever had been fueling it."

She watched the ground race below them. "Won't that be a problem?"

He shrugged his shoulders. "Maybe. We'll see," came his short reply.

She chewed her tongue, wishing he would say more. Was he being secretive, or did he simply not care?

Once they reached the Guardians' condo, the first thing Norah did was take a long shower, never feeling more grateful for electricity in her life. Boston's streets had been hit hard, but the bigger buildings still had power.

She came into the open TV room, towel-drying her hair. A Nature special about jungle ecosystems was playing while Leaf lounged on the couch, sipping hot cider.

"Leaf, your arm!" She pointed. Spidery black veins spread from an angry gash on his shoulder.

"Oh, this?" Leaf rolled his muscular arm. "No biggie; it'll heal eventually." To her, it didn't look like his body was doing anything to heal it.

"It's just some weather demon venom, that's all."

"Uh, shouldn't you get some magical remedy or salve?" she asked.

"That's what I said," added Frost, coming into the open room. He handed her hot chocolate in a candy cane mug.

"Surely the Realm of the Fae has a cure?" she went on.

"Realm of the Fae..." Leaf slowly shook his head.

Frost cleared his throat. "Let him be. If he's content to sulk and do nothing about it, then let him." His arm around her shoulders guided her away.

"You're just going to leave him like that? Won't his mood affect the weather?" she pressed.

"He's good at controlling his emotions. A little moodiness won't hurt anything, but perhaps melt a bit of snow."

She glanced back at the couch, not so certain. But then, what did she know of Guardians? Perhaps they could magically heal themselves with time.

She followed Frost out onto the high, iced-over balcony, the breeze cool, the stars shining in their brilliance and battling against the city lights for attention. Mug warming her hands, she pressed her shoulder against Frost's and fought the urge to lay her head on his shoulder. She wanted to know if he felt the same way about her, if he wanted to share his life with her, and if he would be willing to help her and Tim's situation.

"Frost." She gazed up at him, balancing the mug on the balcony railing. His midnight eyes flicked to her. "Do you like me?"

He regarded her, a softness in his features. "Of course."

"I mean, do you want to be a couple? Start dating...and if things work out, possibly marry...all that?" Her heart hammered wildly in her chest; she thought she might pass out. It was a bold question, but his reaction might tell her what she needed to know.

A shadow crossed behind Frost's expression, almost a sadness or regret, which he quickly masked. His hand rose to brush her cheek. "It's a bit early to jump into such things, Norah. Let's wait until you successfully become the Winter Guardian, and then go from there."

Her gaze lowered, her fingers feeling numb. "Yeah. I guess I was rushing things a bit. We should get to know each other better as friends, anyway." She tried to smile.

He smiled back.

A BIT EARLY TO JUMP INTO THINGS? To even start dating, when he kept acting like he had feelings for her?

Something was off, some piece of the puzzle that she was missing.

Norah wiped the last table clean in The Fast Noodle and stretched her aching arms outward. She needed coffee and a break.

Something crinkled under her foot. She stepped back, stooped down.

It was a piece of paper with a note on it—or rather, drawings.

It couldn't be from Tim; he'd already left with Karin.

A drawing of squiggly lines like a river, and an arrow pointing to a spot near the bridge… Was this a message from Selk?

Bewildered, she pocketed the paper, and before leaving Concord that day, she got her exercise by walking down to the Merrimack River where a highway bridge crossed overhead.

Snow crunched under her boots, sinking her several inches in as she trekked carefully off the path and down to the riverbank. Twigs and high stalks of dead plants shimmered with a crust of ice and snapped as she shoved past.

There, where snow-encrusted ground met ice-edged river, a green head bobbed up out of the water. "Selk, it *was* you!" She hopped down to a patch of white that looked solid enough to hold her weight on the river's edge.

Selk lifted herself the rest of the way out, a gray pelt covering her chest and downward to a seal tail. She reminded Norah of a winter version of a mermaid. "Greetings." Selk turned her torso, bowed her head. "Many sunsets have passed since I saw you last. I'm glad to see the big storm did not harm you."

Norah adjusted her zipped collar awkwardly. "Yeah, we're all doing well enough. Hey, how are the preparations for your clan's migration coming along? Is Leaf trying his best?"

Selk's pale cheeks tinged a shade. "As well as can be hoped for. We are migrating tomorrow. Leaf has been much help; he is as special as a rare black pearl," she replied. "He says it will not be too long of a journey for us. I think the biggest challenge will be adjusting to life in a new place."

"Yeah…" Norah could understand that.

"I hear you are training to be the next Winter Guardian?" Selk asked, tilting her head, water dripping from the ends of her wavy hair strands.

"Yep. It'll be a few years before I can take the job, though.

I've got to get all my life-stuff settled and figured out before then." Norah pocketed her hands in her coat, sitting in a crouch so she wouldn't get a wet snow mark on her pants.

Selk reached and gave her knee a reassuring pat, the blue veins showing in her pale webbed hand. "That is good. Take your time. Frost will be sad to leave you, when the time comes."

Every muscle in Norah stiffened, and her breath stilled.

Frost...leave? What the heck did *that* mean?

"What do you mean, Selk? Frost isn't going to leave. Where would he go?"

Selk's large eyes searched her face curiously. "When a Guardian passes on their power to the new Guardian, they depart this world. That is what Leaf told me."

"Depart? What does that mean, *depart*?" A numb feeling ran down the back of her head and through her limbs.

Selk watched her as if surprised and confused. "Do you not know what a departure is? When a life comes to an end?"

"You can't mean..." Norah's throat seized up. This couldn't be happening. This couldn't be true. There had to be some misunderstanding! Frost said he'd be there by her side, always. They would travel the world together, explore wonders, and...and...

Had it all been a lie?

Her legs suddenly felt weak.

"Norah, are you well?"

Norah managed to stand. "I...I have some things to take care of. It was good seeing you again, Selk. I wish you well on your clan's migration."

Selk nodded. "I wish you well through the winter, Norah."

The rest of the day passed in a surreal blur, Norah finding herself in her car and on the way back to Portsmouth. She barely registered Tim at the table and the dinner Aunt Karin set out for them. She chewed her food mechanically, like a zombie, and stared at the TV until late at night. Then she got ready, sat on the edge of her bed, and waited in the veil of moonlight.

Tim snored quietly.

"It's a bit early to be planning things, Norah. Let's wait until you successfully become the Winter Guardian, and then go from there."

The words spun round in her head.

So *that* was what he'd really meant; that was why he wanted to wait—he knew there would be no future for the two of them!

He'd lied to her, all this time.

Frost's silhouette appeared before the glass. Her numb mind barely registered her legs climbing over the windowsill, his arms catching and lifting her.

Frost took her on an excursion in Boston Harbor. They walked along the cold wooden docks there, and Frost handed her the winter lyre. "Try freezing the moisture on the wood. Then practice icing over parts of the harbor," he told her.

Norah touched her fingers to the strings, but the lyre's song wouldn't come to her, wouldn't guide her fingers. Her mind was too far away. She plucked one string at random and a mournful gust blew past.

Frost's brow furrowed. "Are you sure you're focusing?" He bent to peer at her turned-down face.

She straightened her back and moved to lean against the dock's rails, elbows perched on the wood. Frost watched her, perhaps cautiously, before approaching her side.

"What's gotten you in a sour mood? Was it your mom's boyfriend again?"

Norah squeezed her eyes shut for a moment. "What happens when I take your place as Guardian, Frost?"

He feigned a perplexed expression. "You gain the power to control winter, of course."

"But what happens to *you*?"

To that there was silence. She turned her head to see him go stiff with surprise, like a stealthy animal suddenly caught in a trap. She could tell: he wasn't sure if she knew the truth, and his mind was searching for a way to answer her that wouldn't get him into trouble if she *did* know.

"I...don't understand," was all he could come up with under her scrutinizing stare.

"You'll die, won't you?" she finally stated for him. Her gaze gripped him, and he shifted uncomfortably and tried to look away.

"Why would you think—?" he began.

"Don't try to deny it. Leaf said that's what happens when a Guardian passes on their power." She shifted to fully face him. "You said we would be together. That you'd stay by my side." Tears started to choke her voice, despite her rising anger, her hands curling into fists at her sides. "You gave me hope, a lie... You *lied* to me, Frost! You made me believe that we would share this life together, explore the world together, that I wouldn't be alone... Is it really just you and Leaf, carrying on your work in solitude forever? You want that to happen to me? You want me to suffer and be alone forever?"

Frost gripped the sides of his head as she spoke. And when she asked the last question, he finally shouted, "I can't keep doing this!"

Norah flinched, startled.

He sucked in a breath. "Please, you have to understand what it's been like for me. I had to watch my family age and die, one by one, without being able to be at their side. I had to watch as kids my age enjoyed life, made friends, grew up and...did all the things that I thought *I* would live to do." He exhaled a frustrated breath. "I'm not a real faery, and I'm not human. I don't belong anywhere, and there's no one to share experiences with. This past month has been the most that

I and Leaf have ever interacted." He folded his arms around himself. "I can't do this anymore. I can't...be so alone."

Norah traced him with her gaze. He stood like a shuddering child alone in the dark, and a touch of pity webbed through her anger. "Then why didn't you just tell me that?"

He gave a short, bitter laugh. "Would you have wanted the job if I had?"

She looked away. No, she never would have.

"You don't have to be so alone, Frost. I'm here now. You can spend time with me whenever you need someone."

He just shook his head at the dock's floorboards. "I don't want to watch you grow old and die." His voice came out hoarse.

Norah wiped the edges of her eyes. "Did you ever like me? Did you ever have feelings for me at all?"

Frost kept his head down.

"Or was I nothing to you but your escape plan?" she said as she turned and faced the shore. "Well, I'm done." She started walking away from the docks.

"Norah," Frost called after her. But she didn't look back, and he didn't move to stop her.

She eventually found Leaf and asked him to transport her home. His raised eyebrows showed a question, but he summoned a vortex of leaves and carried her through, back to Portsmouth.

The night felt colder than ever as she tucked into bed. Was it the temperature, or the ache in her chest from a hope dashed to pieces and a bruised heart?

13

FROST'S SOUL REELED INSIDE HIS chest while his feet crossed the condo floorspace. He glimpsed the balcony and paused, imagining Norah there in her puffy coat, hands around a hot mug.

"What on earth did you do?" Leaf's voice struck him from behind. "Don't tell me you went and refused her feelings for you, after all this."

Frost turned around sharply to face him. "She found out that I'll die; *you* told her!"

Leaf looked taken aback for a moment. "I didn't tell… Oh. I had mentioned it to Selk," he realized. "But I never meant for Norah to find out. I mean, not that I'm against her knowing. She *should* know, since it's her life and all."

"You ruined my only chance!" Frost shouted. "Who knows when another human able to replace me will appear? Hundreds of years from now? A thousand?" His foot kicked the back of the sofa.

"Hey, the sofa didn't do anything wrong." Leaf picked up the fallen pillows. His shoulder wound looked worse than yesterday, more blackened. "Somehow, I don't think it's losing your ticket to death that you're so upset about," he said, flicking a glance to Frost. "I think you don't want to lose Norah."

Frost turned and stared at him, mouth dangling open. "D-don't you go assuming things!"

Leaf smirked and gave a shrug. "Either way, calm your temper, before Boston gets flattened by hailstorms." He tossed one of the pillows at him.

Frost smacked the pillow aside and stormed up the glass staircase to his room. City lights glimmered beyond the wide windows near his bed, and he approached his reflection, pressing his forehead to the glass.

It was impossible for them to be together—it *had been* from the start. Either she would die and leave him to suffer alone for countless more centuries, or he would die and enter peace but leave her alone.

What was he supposed to do? What was the right answer?

He pressed his palms to the glass, curls of feathery frost unfurling from his fingertips, and he closed his eyes.

Norah sat up, her body sluggish and tempting her to not do anything else but sleep. Tim wouldn't allow that, though, soon making a ruckus and tugging off her blankets. She groaned.

During breakfast, she hid her heartache and sorrows behind a fake smile.

"It's quite a messy storm out there," noted Karin.

Norah glanced at the window, for the first time noticing. The sky was a heavy gray, and raindrops came down freezing upon whatever surface they touched. The beginnings of an ice storm.

"School's been canceled today," said Karin. "So, relax and waste the day away watching TV or gaming." She winked at them.

Tim bounced in his seat. "It's game time! You won't beat me at Super Smash Bros, Norah!"

Normally she would have hollered back that she'd crush every attack he threw at her, but her heart just wasn't giving her the energy to say anything.

She shouldn't have let her feelings for Frost grow, not without praying about it first—Karin always said to pray about things first. She could have spared herself, and even Frost, from this bitter pain. He must be feeling upset for the clouds to pour such icy rain now, she thought.

Tim poked at her arm. "Why are you quiet?"

Norah shook herself out of her thoughts. "Super Smash Bros, right. You know I always win."

"Not today, you won't!" Tim launched off the chair and scurried across to the TV and gaming console.

"Just give me a minute," she said, pushing off from the table and heading to their shared room. It was time she made an effort to pray, to listen to God instead of to her easily deceived emotions.

"Norah, Tim, I'm heading out to go get some supplies before the storm gets any worse, okay? I'll be right back," Aunt Karin hollered.

The storm grew worse by the minute, and Norah glanced at the wall clock, while steering a purple kart car through a jungle track on the TV. An hour had passed; Karin should be back by now.

She set down the game controller and rose.

"Hey, what gives?" Tim whined and paused the race.

"I'm just going to give Aunt Karin a call." Norah reached for the landline phone Karin still used in her house. Her hand touched the buttons, and in the same moment her cellphone suddenly rang and buzzed in her pocket.

Startled, she pressed the answer button. "Hello?"

"Norah, thank goodness you're at the apartment! Is Tim there with you?"

"Mom? Yes, he's here. What's going on? Why are you calling?"

"The hospital just called me. Karin's been in an accident. I don't know much, but they've just stabilized her condition."

"What?!" Norah couldn't tone down her voice. She saw Tim stand up.

"Calm down. The important thing is that she's alive. I don't know how bad things are yet, but once the storm calms and it's safe to drive, I'll head over to see her. I can pick you up, too."

A shuddering numbness racked through Norah's body. "Yes, do. I can't believe this is happening…" She pressed her hand to her mouth.

"Just stay there, okay? I'll call if I hear anything else."

"Okay, Mom."

"I love you."

"Love you, too."

The call ended.

Tim was watching her intently. "Norah?"

She went over to him slowly, her mind barely able to process the news, her feet moving as if someone else was controlling them instead of her. "Aunt Karin's been in a car accident," she told him. "She's at the hospital."

Tim's face started tearing up and his mouth twisted not to cry.

"It'll be okay. She's alive and safe. We'll go see her soon." She pulled Tim close and let his tears wet her sweater. She rubbed his back and shoulders comfortingly. "Everything will be okay."

She wished she could believe her own words.

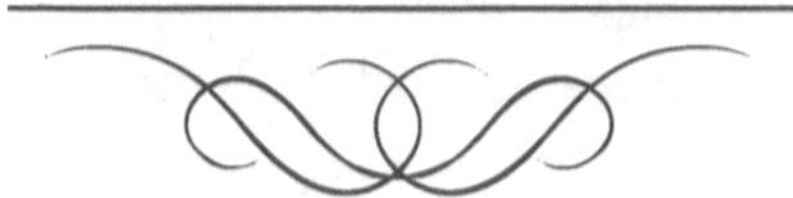

THE STORM DIDN'T LESSEN until the next morning, when Mom picked them up and drove them down to the hospital.

Norah listened to the tap of their shoes down the smooth hallways. Hung paintings along the walls attempted to radiate calm and give a homey feeling to a place that was anything but. And the whole building smelled like cleaning supplies.

A lady at the floor's desk gave them a room number, and Tim dashed ahead to find it. Around a corner, they reached the room, and there inside on one of the beds was Karin, lying still on her back with an IV, bandages and braces around parts of her.

"Aunt Karin!" exclaimed Tim, before Mom could shush him.

Karin's eyes fluttered open and she turned her head towards them. "Ah…you finally made it. About time," she joked, though her state looked nothing to joke about.

"We brought you flowers," said Mom. Norah set them on the bedside table.

Mom motioned for them to find seats and sit down. Tim shifted and fidgeted, full of restless energy and unease.

"So, how bad is it?" Mom asked, taking the blue upholstered chair by Karin's head.

"Ah, well…" Karin glanced about from her to the kids, then to the ceiling, trying to keep a cheerful expression, which instead kept drooping back down. "That ice was so slick on the road after I was done shopping… I shouldn't 've gone out to begin with. But, well, I had to get back home somehow, and the car just didn't want to stay in its own lane, silly thing." She made a sort of cackly laugh.

Mom's serious expression didn't change.

"Anyway," Karin continued, giving up her effort to bring any laughter to the situation. "Doctor tells me I busted up my spine. My legs don't seem to work, no matter how much I try moving them. Still got my arms, though! I can keep brushing my hair, so that's something."

She twiddled her fingers to prove it, but the shock of the news had stunned both Mom and Norah into silence. Tim didn't quite understand the fullness of what this meant, just yet.

"You're paralyzed from the waist down?" Mom's voice came out shaken.

Norah's vision drifted down to the bare floor. The implications had struck her like a wall of bricks. Their home, their life with Aunt Karin, was now over. She and Tim had no place else to go.

Karin waved her hand in dismissal. "Don't you ever watch those medical miracle shows? I could find myself able to walk again, someday! I'm not going to give up on trying, just like that."

Her positive attitude surprised Norah but did little to lift the heavy clouds weighing down upon her shoulders.

After their visit, Mom took them back to the apartment and had them pack their belongings. That was when Tim realized their predicament: that they were going to have to go live with Mom at Bob's place in Boston. Far from Concord. Far from school and her job, which she would no longer be able to keep.

If it hadn't been for that ice storm, none of this would be happening.

If Frost hadn't…

If she hadn't…

Her face fell in her hands as she tried to keep herself together and pray.

Norah recognized the area as soon as they drove up to the sky-high condominium building, the sunset's colors reflecting off of its luxurious glass sides. She sucked in a sharp breath. Bob's condo was directly across from the Season Guardians' condo!

She coughed into her elbow to mask her reaction, Mom giving her an odd look.

Tim had been silent the whole drive, hugging his duffle bag like a pillow. She wished she could offer him comfort, but how much could she give in the face of a living nightmare?

They rode a shiny elevator up to one of the highest floors. Mom kept glancing at the protective arm Norah kept around Tim, shaking her head as if they were both overreacting.

Mom unlocked the door to their condo and shoved it open with her foot. A corridor brought them through the kitchen and living room—a living space that was almost as fancy as the Guardians'.

Bob turned his head from the TV and shifted in his seat on a plush tan sofa. "*Mia bella mama*, you're here," he said, rolling a fake Italian accent at her as if it were sexy. "Oho, and the maggots came with you!" he teased.

Bob's so-called *teasing* was just a way for him to get away with saying demeaning and cruel things, laughing them off as a joke. One of the many things Norah hated about the man.

She didn't meet his eyes, and neither did Tim.

"Where's that spare bedroom?" Mom asked.

Bob rose, a beer in hand, his shirt tight over a bulging stomach. "Left hall, at the end." He pointed with the beer. "I never bother cleaning it, so you'll have fun with that."

Norah ignored the remark, heading down the hall. The last door creaked open, revealing a room with a queen-size guest bed, dusty curtains, and a pile of trash bags needing to be thrown out. The rotten smell permeated the room.

"Oh yeah, forgot to throw those out. Place makes for an easy garbage disposal." Bob laughed over Mom's shoulder and swigged more beer.

Mom gave a forced laugh.

Norah shot her a look, and she cleared her throat. "I'll help pick up," Mom said, grabbing some of the bags and carrying them out while Norah and Tim dragged in their meager luggage.

One bed. They'd have to share.

Karin's apartment was seeming more like a palace by the second, and their old house a royal castle.

Bob leaned against the doorframe, his face smug. They both tried to ignore him. "Listen here, little rats," he said, a finger lifting from the can to point at them. "I'm being more than generous sharing my air with you. So, you make sure and stay out of my way, and give no smart talk. You hear? Food is off limits unless I let you have some. And don't touch anything. This condo and everything in it is worth more than your two pitiful lives combined. I won't be forgiving if something breaks." He tilted his squarish chin down at them, the dim lighting in the room casting an ominous shadow. "We clear?"

"Yes," Norah said shortly, clearing out the single closet that was full of empty boxes.

"And you, boy?" he demanded.

Tim's voice came out tightly, "Yes."

Bob gave them a toothy smirk and sauntered off. "Touch anything in the fridge, and I'll know," he called back.

She heard Tim's stomach growl and saw him lower his head. "Greedy pig," she muttered. "Everybody knows growing kids need food."

They worked until the room was livable and stored their things inside the closet. Tim sat with his knees to his forehead, hungry, and stared longingly at his video game console. There was no TV in this room—and daring to ask to use the one in the living room would be a death sentence.

"My life is ruined," Tim moaned.

Norah rubbed his shoulder. "You'll survive. We both will. I'll find a new job somewhere; places in Boston have better pay, anyway." She tried to sound hopeful.

His stomach grumbled again, and the thought of food made her suddenly hungry, too.

Norah worked on some sketches for her art portfolio through the evening to distract herself, while Tim messed around on his laptop, both of them hiding out in their room and not leaving for anything.

Thick clouds roiled beyond the large window view, their dark underbellies reflecting the glow of the city lights. She set her drawing pad aside and began working her way through the book of Romans in her small Bible from Aunt Karin. She read through chapter 5, verses 8-11.

Her thoughts strayed back to her cheerful aunt: She had grabbed Norah's hand and told her how sorry she was that she could no longer take care of them.

"We're fine," Norah had faked, to put her at ease.

But Karin said, "Take care of your brother and yourself. Don't give up—don't ever do that, Norah. I believe many things happen for a reason, and that there must be a reason for this."

Happen for a reason…

Norah lifted her face, searching for the moon hidden somewhere behind the night clouds.

If only that reason were easy to find…

"Norah, Tim, I brought pizza!" Mom called.

They tried not to show their hurry and eagerness for food, walking quietly out and into the kitchen. Norah took a huge slice of double cheese.

Bob was over in the living room, standing at the wide windows looking out over Boston Harbor, the luxury condo building near to them also in view. He lifted a pair of binoculars to his eyes.

Norah shared a look with Mom.

"Um, honey-sweet, do you want any pizza?" Mom called to the man.

He seemed intent on studying one of the condo flats, blinking and then peering through the binoculars again and again. "There's something strange going on over there, I just know it," he mumbled to no one in particular. "One window is covered in green leaves, and then the next minute it's all frosted over. I look back seconds later, and it's all leaves again! It keeps changing, I tell you. And no matter how hard I try, I can't get a glimpse of whoever's living in the place…"

"Maybe it's haunted," laughed Mom.

A condo with ice and greenery? Uh-oh, it must be *them*. And glamour was keeping Bob from actually seeing *them* but not from seeing what their powers did.

"Haunted…" Bob mumbled indistinctly. "Maybe so, that or else something illegal's going on."

Weeks passed by, with both Norah and Tim finishing up their school semesters online. Norah spent every afternoon looking for a well-paying job that would help her save up money faster, but without a college degree or experience, there wasn't much.

She put her art portfolio up on a freelance artist website, in hopes of getting work that way, and she took a part-time job at a nearby café.

Christmas day had come and gone, with nothing special about it except that Bob threw all his work friends a cocktail party all that night long. She gave Tim her earplugs so that he could sleep, and she let the lull of jazz music on her phone drown out the party noise and drift her into slumber.

Next morning, Norah passed through the kitchen on her way out. Bob was passed out on a couch. The TV had been left on, and the news channel showed images of a large forest fire, started by lightning, that was now spreading across California.

The scene shifted to another disaster: the volcano Bombalai in Malaysia as it erupted without warning earlier that week.

"And let's not forget, David, about Typhoon Masama slowly making its way through the Northwestern Pacific," said a well-dressed lady on screen. "Its winds have already reached 104 knots, and it's showing no current signs of slowing down. The week ahead will be a trying one as both the Philippines and Japan race to prepare for this approaching disaster."

"Yes, there has certainly been an increase in natural disasters around the world, this past month," said David. "We'll continue to monitor the situation, and keep you viewers posted."

The screen shifted to other news, and Norah continued her way out the door.

What were Frost and Leaf doing? Were these new disasters being fueled by them, or were they forced to allow these things to happen?

Frost. She looked to the sky once she was outside. The sky hadn't been clear since the day she parted ways with him. Dreary gray clouds continuously smothered out any blue that tried to show itself.

"Endurance develops strength of character," she repeated the words from a verse to herself, striding across the street and down a block. "I'm going to have a lot of *that* this year."

She put on the café apron, and a part of her missed her coworkers at The Fast Noodle. The afternoon and evening passed quickly, though, with a rush of frustrated customers demanding their coffee and behaving as if their lives depended on the stuff.

"I'll take the caramel swirl latte, hot, with extra caramel syrup, a dash of cinnamon and nutmeg, and extra thick foam on top. Make that a decaf, and with almond milk."

Norah grumbled, writing it all down on a cup, and glanced up at the male customer.

She almost jumped backwards when she saw that it was Leaf—or rather, his human version, all glamourized and not a leaf or moss sprig in sight, wearing a modern and expensive outfit in green shades. He winked at her from behind *Dolce* sunglasses.

"What…the heck," she mumbled. "That'll be five dollars, fifty cents."

Leaf took out his wallet. "Frost needs you," he said in a quiet tone. "It was wrong of him to lie, I know, but taking his place as Guardian would be a far better job for you than...*this*." He motioned at the workstation behind her. "And your brother could live in our condo, if that's what you're worried about. He would have a real home. You wouldn't have to leave him behind or anything."

"Is that true?" She took the cash.

"We used glamour to hide from our families, but your situation doesn't have to be like ours was. You don't have to be invisible to your brother. He's just one person. As long as you feel he can bear the news without his brain exploding, and he agrees to keep the Season Guardians a secret, he can be a part of your life."

"He'll grow old, and I won't."

"Yes...but it might be worth it."

She gave him change back. "Wait at the other line to pick up your coffee." She pointed.

Leaf's lips quirked. "Call me when you change your mind," he whispered to her before shuffling off to the side.

Norah shook her head. At the end of her shift, she dragged her aching feet back to the condo.

She glanced up at the neighboring luxury building as she passed by, seeing if she could spot Leaf or Frost at any of the windows.

Unlocking the polished wooden door with the cardkey Mom had lent her, she entered the flat. Bob lounged before the TV, swigging beer as if it were a daily hobby. Mom's purse was on the table, though she herself wasn't anywhere in sight.

Norah headed to her shared room, and her heart froze at the sound of sniffling.

Only Tim made that sound—and only when something really bad had happened.

Her footsteps hurried to the door and she shoved it open.

There sat Tim on the bed, Mom bending over him and dabbing at his face with a washcloth.

"What the heck happened?" Norah exclaimed. Her purse dropped to the floor as she rushed to Tim's side. Mom drew back with a frown while Norah inspected the bruise around Tim's left eye.

"It's nothing, just an accident," Mom said at the same time as Tim sniffled and managed to say one word: "Bob."

Norah felt her gut flare in anger, and she looked sharply across at Mom. "Are you serious? Bob *hit* him?"

Mom gave a dismissive gesture. "I doubt it's what you think. Bob just had a little too much to drink, and horse-played a bit roughly."

"Horse-play? *That's* what you call this?" Norah came close to shouting.

"Norah, calm down. *Calm down*. You're making too big a deal out of this," Mom said, reaching for her shoulders.

"No!" Norah smacked her hands away. "Abuse *is* a big deal. And I'm not going to tolerate it!"

"Then, what?" Mom shrugged her arms up in the air, exasperated. "Do you have someplace else you can run off to? Do you want the police to come and take your brother away, dump him into a foster home and hope for the best?" She caught Norah by the wrist, her look holding her firmly. "Bob equals money—and that's what you need to survive in this world. Do you want to go to college? Do you want Tim to have a future? Well, Bob can make that happen, if you'll just shut up and tough things out."

"At what cost?" Norah snarled, and jerked her hand free. "Money isn't worth Tim's suffering. Money isn't worth more than his soul or mine." She shoved the closet door open, dragging out their duffle bags.

"What are you doing?" Mom persisted. "You have nowhere to run."

"Tim, pack your things," Norah told him.

Tim hurried to his bag, stuffing the gaming console and other things inside without hesitation.

"Tim, you are *not* leaving. By law, you still have to do what I say." Mom loomed over him.

Norah stood herself between them. "Morals are more important, Mom. And you're too absorbed with your own interests to take care of us anymore."

She grabbed her bag and purse, and Tim followed her out the room and down the corridor.

Mom trailed after, quarreling and whining and flinging every excuse she could think of at them. Tim kept his head down. Bob groaned drunkenly from the sofa and tried to wave one of his arms.

Norah ushered her brother out the flat and over to the elevator.

Mom stopped the doors from closing with her hand. "You can't just leave. I'll call the police! They'll track you down!"

"Good. Then you can explain to them how Tim got this bruised eye, and how Bob is slopping drunk, and you weren't anywhere to help," Norah shot back.

They exchanged heated glares for one drawn moment before Norah pried Mom's hand free and let the elevator door close. Its closing felt like an end to a chapter in their lives.

Tim glanced sidelong up at her. Catchy elevator music played, completely opposite of the current mood. "Where are we going to live?" he asked her, fear hitching his voice.

She wrapped an arm around his shoulders. "I'll take care of you, okay? Trust me. I know what I have to do, now. God's made it clear to me."

Tim's forehead creased with worry, but he nodded and stuck close to her. The night was cold outside the building, and they hurried as quickly as they could. She led him across stretches of grass and paved paths, over to the neighboring and much grander luxury condo and its well-lit front entrance.

"Leaf, I'm here!" she called outside the glass doors, face to the sky, the salty ocean wind whipping her hair and scarf about.

Tim quirked his eyebrows at her.

"Listen to me, Tim. You're going to see things you won't understand, but just trust me. Okay? Don't panic, and just be the cool boy you've always been," she told him at eye-level.

"I'm not panicking—just thinking you've gone a little crazy," he mumbled, huddling in his coat from the chill wind.

A swirl of leaves blew down and Leaf materialized within them. "You called, missy?" His glamour switched off, and she watched Tim's jaw drop to his chest, his thoughts most likely mirroring what her own had first been.

Leaf flashed Tim a grin, and the vines curling in his auburn hair twitched their small leaves.

"Tell Frost I'm taking the job. And…that we need a place to live," she said, the cold shivering her voice.

"Well, don't just stand there turning into icicles. Hurry inside!" Leaf ushered them indoors to the foyer, glamouring on his human disguise for the other residents to see.

15

TIM DASHED FROM ONE OPEN room to the next, like a kid who'd just discovered wonderland, dragging his bag behind him all the way. His mouth hung wide open, his eyes taking in the glass staircase and chandeliers and the high ceiling above. He halted his exploration when Frost appeared, the ice guy's shoes clicking down the glass stairs.

Frost adjusted his fine white shirt collar. "What do we have here? Are we running some sort of charity?" When he reached the lower floor, he shifted his attention away from Tim and with a start saw Norah, there beside Leaf.

"Hi," she said nervously, with a small wave. He took slow, apprehensive steps, looking back and forth between the two of them. "I've been thinking things over, and…I'd like the

Winter Guardian job," Norah said, fiddling her hands together and feeling her cheeks heat. "But only on one condition: my brother lives here with me."

Frost stood facing her for one moment; she could see the emotions at war within him. Then he gave her a brief nod of assent. "I'm fine with that. It's Leaf who's going to have to live with this decision, though."

Leaf rolled his eyes. "Believe me when I say these two will be more cheerful to live with than you've ever been."

Frost came closer to her, pocketing his hands. "Can I ask what changed your mind?" Clearly, he'd noticed the bruise on Tim.

"I want to be free, just as much as you do," was the answer she gave.

After a silent pause, he nodded his head to the side. "Go pick a guest room; there are two."

Tim dashed off excitedly, and Norah followed with her duffle bag.

Later, when they came back to the kitchen area, Leaf served up a pasta casserole and veggie dish, and Tim stuffed himself as if he'd just come out of a famine—which, in a way, was true for both of them. Overall, he seemed to be taking the strangeness of everything rather well.

"How did the selkie migration go?" Norah asked Leaf, taking note of his still injured shoulder.

"Ah, very well!" Leaf set down his wine glass. "I had to scare off a few sharks and orca along the way, but the clan made it into the bay safely. They've got more fish there to eat than they know what to do with!"

Tim quirked an eyebrow. "Selkies are real? Whoa."

Leaf gave him a wink. "About as real as I am." A small vine snaked across the table towards Tim, wrapping around his fork and lifting pasta up to his mouth.

Tim grinned and wrestled the fork away from the vine.

It felt good to see his full smile again, Norah thought.

After dinner, Frost handed them each a mug of hot cocoa. Tim went to the TV area with Leaf, fascinated by the luxurious décor and the giant screen TV that was easily five times bigger than what they were used to.

"You fought off orcas? How did you survive? And how does moss grow on your skin? Tell me everything!" While Tim released a flood of questions, Norah watched him from a distance in the living room and briefly smiled.

"Norah, can I talk to you?"

She turned to Frost. The memory of hurt between them made her want to refuse, sink into herself and hide, but he strode over to the balcony door, waiting for her.

She exhaled and followed him outside.

It should have been windy this high up, but it felt as if an invisible shield kept the wind from touching them. The clouds had finally parted, letting the moon's soft white glow shine through. She closed her hands tighter around the hot mug, which featured a flattering depiction of Jack Frost from a movie.

She looked from the mug to him. "Really?"

He shrugged. "What? Can't I collect my own memorabilia?"

"*This* Frost has white hair and is way nicer," she jabbed.

Frost rolled his eyes dramatically. "Well then, find me hair dye and a staff, and I'll do my best to please you."

She tried to suppress the impish smile on her lips.

Suddenly embarrassed, she cleared her throat and spoke to fill any possible silence. "I hear there are many natural disasters happening around the world, right now. Shouldn't you and Leaf be busy stopping them?"

He regarded her with a sideways look. "I've been preventing many of them," he replied. "But they keep popping up like weasels, again and again, and I can't figure out why… I just hope it's not because of me."

"What, you've been stressed out since I left?" she half joked.

He didn't answer. And she cleared her throat.

"You know that big ice storm that ran through New England? Well, my Aunt Karin got in a car crash because of it, and now she can't walk." Sudden tears pricked her vision in the cold. "We had to move in with my mom's fiancé, and…it's been a nightmare." Her tone made it clear that she put part of the blame on Frost.

The edges of his eyes creased as if pained. "I had no idea, Norah. I'm sorry. I failed to control my thoughts that day, and the weather got out of hand… I have no excuses. I can pay the medical bills and for physical therapy," he offered.

Norah took a gulp of hot chocolate, letting it wash away the chill. "I'll take that offer," she said.

Silence ticked by for a while between them.

"What I wanted to say to you is…I'm sorry. For lying, for hurting your feelings, and for…*everything*. I let fear rule my judgement, and that made me turn selfish." Frost couldn't face her as he spoke but stared out over the cityscape. "I ended up hurting myself, too, as…" he swallowed, "as my feelings for you grew."

Norah's lips parted and she tried to smother her racing heart from feeling anything. "Saying sorry can't fix everything," she mumbled.

He lowered his chin. "No. But I hope that my actions from now on can help."

She glanced sidelong at his shoes: feathers of frost wove across the black leather like diamond lace. "Thanks for letting us stay," she finally said. "I'll work hard training with the winter lyre tomorrow."

His lips finally curved a smile, if briefly. It felt genuine this time, and beautiful.

Back inside the living room, he handed her the lyre from its seat on a frozen chair. "Keep it with you for a day. Get used to the feel of having it around," he told her. "But don't lose it," he warned with a mock seriousness.

She barked a single laugh. "I never lose anything." She lifted her chin in full confidence.

"I hope not. Here's my precious debit card, in case you need something." He took it out and gave it a parting kiss before handing it over, as if he might never see it again.

"Oh please," she mock sighed. Though, having that much money in the palm of her hand for the first time in her life did make her knees slightly quiver.

Frost stayed awake long after Norah and her brother went off to bed. He didn't need to sleep, though occasionally he allowed himself to.

He leaned against the ceiling-high windows of the living room, watching a sliver of golden dawn breach the ocean horizon line.

Leaf closed the fridge and came over to his side to join in admiring the view. He handed him a glass of sparkling cider and surveyed the sky's night veil as it gradually rolled away. "Things worked out in the end, didn't they?" he said cheerfully. "All that moping and sulking you did for the past three weeks was all for nothing!"

His grin pricked Frost the wrong way.

Frost sniffed and raised his chin. "I wasn't sulking. Sad, yes. But I wasn't being a baby about it."

"Fine, Mr. Not-baby."

"And for your information, me dying while Norah has to live on is not what I would call *things working out in the end*," he voiced moodily.

"Oo-hoo! You're finally being honest with yourself, are you? Finally admitting that you like Norah." Leaf waggled a finger at his cheek teasingly.

"Shut up." Frost sidestepped away from his annoying reach and tipped the cider into his mouth. "That's not getting any better, you know." He indicated with the glass the wound on Leaf's shoulder. "Go visit the Nymph of Seasons and get it healed."

The merriment faded from Leaf's eyes, though his face still held a grin. "Maybe later," he said. "I have some pressing work to do, first."

The room suddenly swayed beneath Frost's feet.

He stumbled, and used his free hand to rub at his forehead, slick with sweat beneath his fingers. "What...?" He tried to put down the glass. Missing the coffee table, it shattered on the ice-encrusted rug. "What's wrong with me?"

Leaf watched him, not moving an inch. His grin fell into a cold curl of the lips, all his merriment gone like a tossed-away mask. "Even though we never did get along much, I'm still sorry it had to come to this," he said, though no expression of regret or anything else showed on his face.

"You...what have you done?" Frost struggled to speak through the fog that was filling his head. He felt his knees hit the floor.

"I tried to keep the Winter Guardian successor at bay, all those years ago—tried to prevent him from reaching the cave and the Winter Dome, where the old Winter Guardian awaited. The storm I had summoned succeeded in doing that. But then *you* showed up, ruining my plan and taking the old man's place as the new Winter Guardian."

"What...are you talking about?" Frost tried to follow his words.

"I want to end winter, Frost. Put an end to it for good," Leaf finally stated.

The vines crawling down his bare arms curled angrily.

Frost could barely comprehend what he was hearing. Was this really Leaf, or an imposter? He reached for the table to steady himself, but instead his head slumped against the rug.

"It's been my goal for a very long time, now. I've been waiting patiently. And now, without the winter lyre in your grasp, and with your mind weak and distracted, the perfect time that I've been waiting for has come."

Leaf's words became distant to his ears; the rug and the ceiling and lights became a fuzzy darkness.

"*My* time…has come…" the words echoed.

16

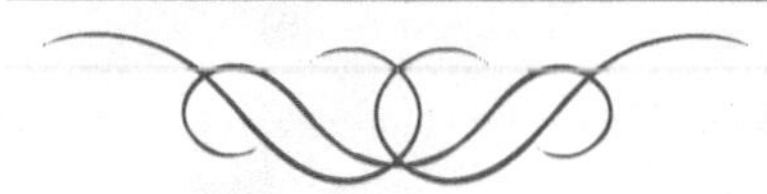

FROST LIFTED HIS CHEEK FROM THE mossy floor, and daylight and the world came back into focus around him.

But it wasn't the condo that he woke up at.

Vines wove and crawled over the stone wall surfaces of the room. Thick moss carpeted the rock floor, speckled with flowers, and jungle moss dangled from an ancient domed ceiling overhead. Shafts of light slanted in through narrow window gaps, high up near the dome.

And there, at the center of this strange room, stood a great throne made of living wood and blossoming roses.

This was the Summer Dome, a twin to the Winter Dome where he had become the next Winter Guardian.

Here, in this place, summer's power was at its strongest.

Frost lifted his hand, summoning a coating of ice to form, yet nothing happened. He tried to gather the power of winter, but not even a chill breeze answered his call.

Frost forced his groggy body to stand, and he stumbled his way over to the towering entrance doors, made up of thickly woven tree roots.

He pulled on the wooden handles, but they were sealed shut.

He was trapped. And with him, winter was locked away.

"The typhoon…the volcanic activity…the sudden rising storms." It all made sense, now. It hadn't been Frost's doing—well, the snow and ice weather had been, but not the destructive forces of nature that would soon grow and ravage the lands.

"It was Leaf, all along. His anger is what's fueling the weather demons."

Leaf had waited for Frost to hand over the winter lyre to Norah, because a Guardian couldn't steal another's power channeler. But now that Norah had it, who wasn't yet a Guardian, Leaf could take it from her.

He slammed his fist against the doors. "Leaf, you idiot! You've thrown the seasons out of balance, and now the Earth will be destroyed!"

He pounded against the woven root doors, shouting again and again, yet no answer came.

Norah walked to work early that morning. Heavy clouds of an unusual green haze were choking out the sun, and a warm wind speckled with drizzle blew across her face and ran through her hair.

Warm air in winter?

She looked up at the gathering storm overhead. "I don't know much about Boston weather, but I'm pretty sure the clouds never turn green or warm in January," she spoke aloud.

Thunder rumbled and the wind picked up. She dashed under the awnings of shops on her way to the café.

When her shift began, few customers were risking the wind and growing darkness to come get a coffee. And after just one hour in, cellphones throughout the café started ringing with a tornado watch alert.

"Okay, we're closing up shop!" announced the manager. "Customers aren't coming in, anyway. Get home before this storm gets any worse."

"Who ever heard of a tornado watch in Boston?" one coworker was saying.

Another nodded vigorously. "Did you feel the air? It's like a tropical storm brewing out there!"

Norah hurried to change and get her things. The winter lyre sat snug in her coat's long inner pocket. "Oh Frost, don't tell me you let Leaf trick you into drinking too much wine or something. Are you drunk?" she muttered.

She texted Tim to head downstairs to the condo building's lobby and wait there for her—that had to be safer than waiting inside the sky-high flat with a possible tornado approaching.

Damp wind struck her the moment she stepped outdoors. She yanked her blue hood up.

It *did* feel like a warm storm blown in from the south. How strange. Frost usually made cold weather—not warm weather.

She forged ahead on foot, bracing herself, and after a while, the city streets faded behind her as the luxury condo's pristine common grounds came into view. The winter-bare trees along the drive were bending in the strong wind gusts.

A figure hovered in the air not far from her. Small creatures like sprites with leafy wings and twig-like bodies eddied around the person.

"Go throughout the northern lands," the figure spoke, "to the east and west, and spread the warmth of summer. Awaken the flora and fauna from their slumber! Winter no longer rules."

It was Leaf, she realized.

Before she could comprehend what was happening, Leaf descended. His feet landed with a mossy bounce upon the path before her.

"Norah, where is the winter lyre?" he asked. His clay-colored eyes gave off a cold intensity, contrasting the cheer of his lips.

"I…" She stopped her hand from moving, and gripped the collar of her coat instead. "I put it somewhere safe. Why? Does Frost need it? How did this storm pop up out of nowhere?" she asked, trying not to sound nervous.

Leaf's pleasant smile lowered bit by bit. "He needs the lyre to calm this storm. Here, hand it over and I'll fly it up to him." He held out his hand.

Something was off. There was an angry bitterness shining behind his gaze and stiff posture, very unlike the Leaf she had come to know.

She shook her head. "I'll go get it and hand it to him myself," she said. She moved to walk around him.

He stepped in her way.

"Tell me where it is," he demanded in an even tone. Black veins had spread down his arm from the shoulder wound.

Why was Leaf doing this?

"Why won't you let me take it to Frost myself? Where is he?" she demanded. "I didn't see either of you this morning."

A shadow crossed Leaf's features and his hand shot out.

Norah jumped back several steps out of reach. "What's happened to you?" she exclaimed.

"Give me the winter lyre, Norah, and I'll leave you alone," he demanded, stepping forward. "You can keep the condo—everything will be paid for—and you and all the humans of earth can enjoy a warmer world. The seasons of spring and summer will dominate; no more bite of winter chill will exist."

He reached out again. She backed away several more steps and her mouth gaped in shock. "Are you *crazy*? You're trying to get rid of winter?" she exclaimed.

"That's right. This planet used to be all warmth and greenery, long ago, you know—or so the ancient texts say. I simply want to return the earth back to the way it should be."

Norah went around a tree, spacing its trunk between them. "Even if it once was, that's not how the world can be anymore! Do you realize how many creatures will die without the cold and snow? How many islands and communities will be submerged under water if all the polar ice melts?"

Leaf didn't seem to be listening, his eyes glazed over with only one goal in mind.

"What about Selk? Can she survive in tropical waters?"

Leaf's advance paused for a moment. "I will help them adjust. I will help all the creatures adapt. This is what's best for everyone, Norah, it'll improve the world. Can't you see that? No more snow and ice means no more danger on the roads, no risk of freezing to death for the homeless, no more dying crops or lack of food... No more accidents, like with your Aunt Karin."

Norah couldn't swallow. She suddenly recalled, in a flashback, that evening back when Leaf had told them how he'd become the Summer Guardian.

"*...I was able to watch my siblings grow up from afar... That is, until a vicious ice storm caused their vehicle to crash.*"

She remembered the anger hidden there, buried deep inside him. Now it was free, bursting forth like lava and fueling him.

"All this time, you've been wanting revenge for your siblings' deaths," she said, astounded. "Why didn't you tell us? If you'd shared your feelings and been honest, we could have helped you."

"Helped me *how*?" he interrupted and snarled. "By convincing me to move on and ignore their deaths, is that what you mean? Because I refuse to do that any longer. I will make this world a better place, in memory of my family." He rounded the tree. "Now, hand over that lyre!"

Norah grabbed the lyre out from her jacket and strummed the strings.

A sharp gust of cold knocked Leaf back several paces.

"Where is Frost?" she yelled at him.

Blackened veins webbed up his collarbone to his neck as she watched. "Locked away, until he withers and winter is no more," came his bitter answer.

Norah's pulse pounded. She couldn't let the lyre fall into Leaf's hands, and yet she was nothing but a weak human.

Plucking three strings, she summoned a burst of snow like a flowing curtain to cover his face, blinding his vision. She turned and ran.

What should she do? Who could help her find Frost?

Leaf had summer sprites, and Frost had mentioned the little winter ones, once before. But would they come at her call? How could she call them?

Thinking of the winter sprites, what she imagined them to look like, she felt along the lyre's strings, letting the instrument guide her fingers to make an undulating tune.

The air above her head swirled suddenly, a vortex opening up, and white creatures with icy crystal wings poured through.

"Help me! Take me away from here!" She raised her arms high to them.

They blinked glassy eyes at her, then flew in an eddy

around her body.

"I won't let you stop me, Norah!" screamed Leaf. He charged across the path, moss making his feet glide more than run.

"Please!" she cried to the sprites.

As one, they seemed to come to a decision and wrapped around her. Then they lifted her up into the vortex of wind and snowflakes.

NORAH'S FEET HIT THE GROUND. Her arms pinwheeled to steady herself, and then she turned her head this way and that, looking around at where the snowy vortex had dumped her.

A foot from her stood the bronze mother duck of the *Make Way For Ducklings* row of statues in Boston's Public Garden. Heavy raindrops fell in a slow patter, and warm gusts of air battered the trees and her coat. Patches of clouds overhead were rotating and bulging, threatening to become tornadoes at any moment.

The winter sprites flew in a spiral around her, their crystal-like eyes taking her in and examining the lyre—probably wondering why *she* had it, and not Frost.

"Frost is in trouble. I have to find him! Can you help me do that?" she begged them. "Can you sense where he is?"

One of the sprites began to nod, and then all of their heads were nodding, like a school of synchronized fish.

She got out her phone, quickly thumbing a text to Tim:

Stay with the people in the lobby. If they evacuate to a shelter, go with them. Something's happened to Frost. I have to go help him, I don't know how long I'll be. Hide from Leaf, don't let him find you. I'll call when everything's settled. If you need help, contact my Velvet Café coworkers. Love you!

"Okay, winter sprites." She pocketed her phone and held the lyre close. "Take me to Frost!"

Her body and vision submerged into the snowy vortex once more. She held her breath instinctively, the whirl of darkness and air pressure feeling too much like drowning for comfort.

Fear pricked up her spine while she was carried through the swirling, near-black tunnel that had no visible end. It was a good thing her old, cramped house had cured her of ever feeling claustrophobic, she thought wryly to herself.

The vortex suddenly broke apart and vanished into a sea of daylight, and she dropped like an injured bird out of the clouds.

The sprites pulled on her coat, slowing her fall to the grassy ground below.

She stood upon a rolling plain. The air was cool and damp from a storm brewing overhead, and the vibrant green shrubs and lull of the landscape looked nothing like New England.

Where was she? She thought.

Wait, didn't Frost once mention something about him first becoming a Guardian on the shores of Ireland? Wow, was she actually standing in the land of faery lore?

A winter sprite tugged on the cuff of her sleeve, pulling her arm eastward away from the late sun.

"You want me to walk over there? But there's nothing around here for miles," she told the creature.

It didn't make sense to her, but she chose to listen and followed the group of sprites as they led her along like a school of air fish. She trekked up and over one of the many hills, tufts of grass tugging at her shoelaces.

"There's still nothing here," she grumbled, following the creatures up the side of a second hill.

On the other side, going down, she had to watch her step; the steeper slope and damp grass were making a treacherous combination.

After slipping and sliding several times, she managed to reach the base and steadied herself. There, pressed into the side of the hill, stood a stone almost as tall as she was, and with a spiral symbol of a sun engraved in detail across its surface.

She peered closely at the strange symbol.

The winter sprites' wings made a buzzing squeak. One of them kept tapping on the stone and then pulling at her fingers.

"Okay, okay!" She pressed her hand to the stone, and waited.

Nothing happened.

Their wings buzzed impatiently at her.

"I don't know what you want me to do!" She groaned exasperatedly.

The wind picked up, rushing down the rolling landscape and threatening to blow them all away. Norah ducked against the hill's side.

If winter and the balance of seasons were not returned soon, the world would become a chaos of storms and natural disasters.

Leaf would probably arrive here any minute and stop her, too, once he figured out the winter sprites could follow Frost's trail.

Unsure what else to try, she slipped out the winter lyre from her coat and touched it to the stone.

The stone glowed to life upon contact, and in silence it swung itself open.

A doorway.

Norah peeked inside.

A bolt of lightning struck the ground several yards away, back behind her, flinging up soil and thundering mightily.

Leaf was coming.

The sprites shoved Norah into the dirt tunnel, though they did not dare to enter it themselves, being made of winter as they were. So, she made her way through the tunnel and into a glowing cavern beyond: made of stone surfaces covered in mysterious patterns of swirls and braids, and carpeted in feathery moss. At the heart of the magical cavern rose a green, domed structure, decorated in more symbols of the sun.

It became clear that this must be the home of Summer: the place where new Summer Guardians were made, and where summer power was at its strongest.

The perfect cage for winter.

She raced across the mossy floor of the cavern. Shafts of light somehow penetrated the hill's surface, above, to cast a shine down across the dome's emerald stonework.

A series of steps covered in a carpet of woven flowers led up to the structure's grand doors. The doors were made of woven tree roots, thick, knotted and sinuous.

"Frost, are you in there?" she called, and pressed her ear to the roots.

She could hear a muffled sound, like a suffocating voice trying to be heard, but the door was too thick.

Norah grabbed a jutting piece of root like a door handle

and pulled. Nothing budged.

She pushed against the root door with all her weight.

Still nothing.

She stared hard at the thick roots for a while. Not even the touch of the lyre, nor a song from its strings, made the doors shift when she tried. And worst of all, she could hear the humming of the winter sprites back beyond the tunnel, a humming of panic and urgency.

Leaf was here. If she didn't open these doors now…

She backed up, scanning every inch of the structure. There were small gaps like windows just beneath the dome ceiling. But the height…

She hurried to a wall and the vines that crawled up it. There was no more time to think.

Rekindling her bravery and sense of adventure, she began the climb up the ropey vines, like she would have a tree when she was little—a very tall tree; she had to ignore the drop of forty feet below.

Reaching one of the window-like gaps, her fingers gripped the ledge, and she pulled herself up just enough to peer through into the large room within and call out. "Frost, up here!"

Frost's head turned at her voice, his expression going wide in surprise. "Norah! How did you find me?" His fair skin looked faded, dull, the snowflakes on his hair and clothes half melted, almost gone. Even so, his gaze showed a deep fondness and relief to see her.

"Save the questions for later." She lowered a rope-like branch of vine down to him that she'd yanked loose. "I'm assuming your power to fly doesn't work inside there?"

"How ever did you guess?" He smirked. He grabbed on and pulled himself up, hand over hand, feet crossed for leverage.

Just when he reached the top, the root doors to the Summer

Dome unraveled and opened, and Leaf stormed through. His gaze swept the room once, then lifted, latching on to Frost who was squeezing himself through the open gap.

"Frost!" he bellowed.

Frost hoisted his torso then legs out of the gap, and clung to the jungle of growing vines along the outside wall. Norah passed him the winter lyre with her free hand. His face lit up, and a spark of power returned to his dulled skin. The snowflakes covering him reshaped, whole once more.

He let go of the vines and his body hovered in the air. He reached down and lifted her up in one arm.

"You're not going to ruin my long-awaited plan this time, Frost!" shouted Leaf, as he raced around the Dome to catch them.

Frost soared high over the Dome and dove down toward the exit tunnel carrying her.

Leaf also took flight and lunged, his hand barely missing Frost's heel as they all hurtled through the corridor of dirt and out into daylight—or rather, into the gloomy gray of a roiling storm.

Leaf disappeared somewhere behind them.

Frost didn't pause; he continued to fly over miles of green hills and landscape until an Irish town came into view. There, he lowered and dropped Norah on her feet. "Keep safe indoors. Don't go anywhere for any reason until this is all over," he urged her. "Thank you for saving me, Norah. I know you want to be of more help, but this is a battle between Guardians now." He brandished the lyre like a weapon.

"Frost..." she began worriedly.

"I won't lose." He flashed her a determined smile. His finger brushed a strand of her hair, tucking it behind her ear.

And then, he was gone, soaring off into the clouds.

18

FROST SOARED THROUGH THE RAGING, frothing storm. Flashes of lightning lit up the edges of the clouds every few seconds around him. Then, one such flash outlined a humanoid shape, hovering not far away.

"Stop what you're doing, Leaf, and we can put all of this behind us," Frost called out, giving him one last chance.

Leaf's bitter laugh reverberated through the heavy atmosphere and condensation. "*You're* the one who needs to stop, Frost. Winter must die. Let the Earth be free of your cold grasp!"

The summer flute whistled at his lips, and a bolt of lightning forked towards Frost.

Frost summoned a wall of ice in the air just in time—the ice absorbing the impact and shattering at the powerful heat's touch.

Leaf charged forward, his body phasing in and out of the clouds and mist surrounding them. A mass of vines shot out like snakes, seeking to entangle Frost.

Frost swerved left, down, then upward to the right as he dodged, the vines unable to grab him but instead striking him like whips and covering him in welts.

He strummed the winter lyre, summoning a sword of ice in his right hand. He slashed and hacked one-handedly, severing the vines.

But the more vines he severed, the more vines took their place, and the strength of his arm was wearing down.

A harsh chord of the winter lyre sounded, and a shell of protective ice wrapped around Frost and sharp spikes jutted out from it dangerously.

The attacking vines were shredded against the spikes. Leaf drew them back to himself, his lip curled in a snarl. A wave of icicles formed in the clouds, and they cut through the air like a volley of arrows at him.

Leaf grew a shield of wood from his arm, blocking the projectiles. Icicles cut into the wood, but others stabbed at his unprotected legs. He gritted his teeth.

The summer flute whistled, and another fork of lightning arced toward Frost. The ice shell around him shattered like glass on impact.

Frost held his forearms up to cover his face, the breaking noise sharp in his ears, and he blinked his eyes repeatedly to get rid of the lightning's afterimage warping his vision. He flew backwards away and up into thicker cloud cover.

Leaf followed, the stab wounds in his legs dripping blood.

From higher in the atmosphere, Frost could feel the turmoil of the earth: the northern hemisphere heating up; the storms in the oceans growing wilder; the shifting of the earth's crust sparking new earthquakes.

This all had to be stopped soon, or else…

Frost wrapped himself in ice once more, but this time in the shape of plates of armor. He stopped his ascent near the top of the thunderstorm, and the lyre's song formed an army of hailstones.

Leaf appeared from below, and Frost fired the swarm of hailstones down.

Leaf quickly wrapped himself in wooden armor. Hailstones bounced off it and chipped away chunks of wood. The flute rose to his lips and he summoned a long chord of hot white: a lightning fire whip.

Frost summoned the ice sword again quickly, blocking the whip's oncoming attack. The burning heat of its viper-like tongue seared his cheek before it coiled back in the air.

Frost flew into a dive at Leaf, sword ready, striving to reach him before the fire whip could finish its recoil and lash out again.

Leaf's eyes glowed with rage, his hand trying to pull the fiery whip back into another attack.

But Frost reached him first, and a stray beam of sunlight slanted through the top of the storm to glint off his armor and the sharp tip of the ice sword.

The sword swung, and Leaf bent sideways to avoid its swipe.

But it wasn't Leaf he was aiming for.

The summer flute cracked in two, divided by the sword's edge.

Leaf's wide gaze went from the sword to the now severed flute drifting down out of his grasp through the clouds below.

Frost's sword arm was still moving from the swing, when he felt a tug in his other arm and a hot burning pain.

The fire whip's tip had curled itself around the bow of the

winter lyre. And before Frost could react, the whip gave a sharp yank, and the heat snapped the lyre's crossbar and strings clean off.

"NO!"

Frost watched as the dead lyre fell away, along with the flute.

He lifted his gaze through his eyelashes, meeting Leaf's heated glare.

Their anger smoldered for one moment, and then they flew at each other in pure rage, all caution and tactics thrown aside.

They met—burning fist to ice-hard knuckles, in a brawl of gut punches and face kicks and the tearing off of both wood and ice armor.

Frost bled from a split lip, his body a work of welts and burn marks. Leaf showed a bruised eye socket and bloody limbs, and the black veins were still stark across his shoulder and collarbone.

Lightning flashed, unrestrained, across the skies of Ireland and over the whole of the United Kingdom. Bouts of hail rained down, unbidden, and the winds picked up, rotating in the threat of multiple tornadoes. Without the lyre and flute to control and channel their power, the forces of both summer and winter tore loose across the earth.

The higher he and Leaf soared in battle, the more devastation became visible beneath them. They reached the line where atmosphere and the nothingness of space met, and Frost grabbed Leaf's blackened arm, spinning him around and pinning the arm behind him in a firm hold.

"This has to stop!" Frost shouted in his ear. "Look—look down there at what you've done. Who knows how many weather demons you've fueled? And now the temperature of Earth is changing drastically, with no seasons to hold it in place!"

Leaf had no choice but to look as Frost held him.

A massive typhoon was blowing over the Philippines, in a whirl of devastation, and the tips of its rotating arms were reaching for Japan next.

Two giant hurricanes barreled their way across the Atlantic, threatening to wipe out entire islands and wash away American coastlines.

A massive fire torched lands, farms, and houses as it spread through California, showing no signs of slowing down as it was carried farther and farther by the dry fuel of summer heat. And there were more fires to match it blooming all across the country and up into Canada.

Volcanoes along the Ring of Fire began to wake from their slumber. The larger ones puffed smoke and ash that sent entire populations running in terror for their lives. Just one massive volcanic eruption could be enough to cover the world in darkness and famine for several years—as had happened before in Earth's ancient history.

And that wasn't even taking into account the polar vortexes that were now brewing a mixture of cold and heat at the North and South Poles. The coming devastation would be catastrophic, and there would be no recovering from it.

The Earth was warming—and at a price of lives that could never be worth it.

As the realization hit him, Leaf's eyes finally dimmed of their furious light.

"There won't be hardly anyone left alive to enjoy your new world, Leaf," Frost said to drive the point home. He shoved him away, letting him go.

Leaf hovered there, staring down at the planet, his jaw quivering.

"Look, I'm sorry about what happened to your family all those years ago. But it wasn't my doing, nor anyone else's, and you can't keep looking for someone to blame. This is a fallen world where people die—whether it be by ice storm or something else—and there's nothing we can do to change that until the End Days. I wish I could say something more comforting…but the truth doesn't always give comfort." Frost sucked in a breath, thinking back to his own family long since gone.

"I'm going to the Nymph of Seasons for help," Frost told him. "You can either come with me or stay out of my way."

Frost flew off, heading for the point of space that hovered above the British Isles: the dimensional pocket of the Hall of Seasons. Behind him, Leaf followed, his expression grim.

The Hall doors opened, letting them inside to the grand display of the four seasons, far grander and purer representations than anything currently found on Earth. Frost hurried down the long center floor.

"Lady Seasons, Lady Seasons!" Frost called out as he jogged. "We need your help!"

He reached the ornate, seasons throne and slowed to a halt. "Lady…?"

The far door melted itself open, and the Nymph of Seasons entered through, her liquid body and fluid dress rippling like water. Flower petals fell from the blossoms blooming on her birch wood antlers.

"It is about time you came," she spoke. "Why did you wait so long, when the Earth is in such a dire state?" Her tone berated Frost.

He lowered his head. "I thought I could handle things on my own… Forgive me," he answered, feeling heavy with regret.

She lifted a finger to touch his forehead, and a flow of energy rolled over him. The welts and injuries on his body healed, and the blood dissolved away.

Her liquid gaze then turned to Leaf, who stood several paces back. "Leaf, come forward." Her voice echoed through the Hall with an edge.

Leaf kept his head down as he moved his feet, coming around Frost.

"Closer," she commanded.

Leaf reached the base of the throne dais where she stood, every inch of him uneasy.

Her gaze swept over him from head to toe, making Leaf break out in a nervous sweat. "You took it upon yourself to alter the course of the world, as if it was yours to alter," she said.

Leaf's feet stood planted apart, his hands behind his back and gripped together.

"You were given this power as a privilege to serve Lord God's creation. Have you forgotten that this power does not belong to you?"

Leaf's gripped hands trembled now, as Frost watched from a pace back.

"What do you have to say for yourself?" she asked.

Leaf stared at the floor where her liquid dress met the transparent glass tiles. "I let my anger and arrogance get the better of me." He finally admitted, quietly. "I let revenge become more important to me, and I didn't care how everyone else would be affected. I…thought I knew what was best for the world."

Her head shook slowly, a rain of petals cascading down. "None of us knows what is truly best for the world, Leaf. The scope of it is too great for us to fully comprehend. That is something only the Creator's vast knowledge can determine."

She lifted her hand, indicating his arm. "An injury made by evil cannot be healed on your own. It has festered and tainted you, magnified the bitterness already present in your heart. You should have come to us, right away."

"I told him so," Frost muttered.

Leaf had enough spirit left to shoot a glare over his shoulder at him.

"Come." The Lady's arm gestured to the shimmering door, and Leaf followed her.

"Wait, Lady Seasons. I can't just wait here. Let me go down to Earth and restore winter," Frost pleaded. "The winter lyre and summer flute are broken. But is there something I can use in its place?"

The Nymph turned, the dress becoming like a waterfall around her. Her palms raised, and the space in between them burst with a flash of brilliant light.

Frost squinted, and when he looked again, there the winter lyre hovered: fully restored. She sent it floating across the air to his outstretched hands.

"But how…?"

"Did you think there was something broken of yours that could not be fixed? Go, now. Carry your responsibility and restore winter."

Frost bowed and hurried out of the Hall of Seasons.

19

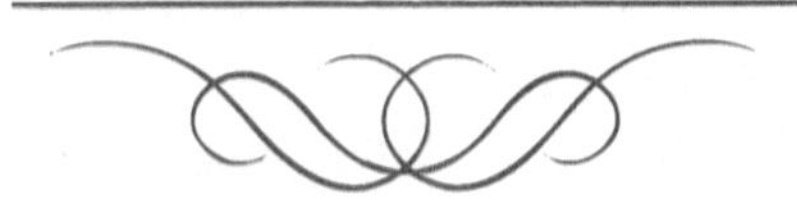

FROST RACED TO THE NORTHERN polar region, where warm air was colliding and mixing with the frigid cold and brewing up a storm so great that, if not stopped, would threaten all the northern countries surrounding it and beyond.

Massive chunks of ice were breaking away to become icebergs in the deep ocean beneath him. He flew across to a landscape of ancient, rugged ice, and there played the winter lyre.

A deep song of cold and ocean waves flowed from the lyre, a lulling cadence that made firm the cliffs of white and ceased the breaking of icebergs, sewing together the melting cracks.

The howling winds of the storm slowed in their rage, and Frost plucked the strings to lower the air temperature back to its below-freezing state and dried up any remaining warmth into a chill.

His body felt exhausted by the time the northern polar region's climate was restored to normal. And yet, there were still so many storms and the chaotic southern polar region left to deal with.

Restoring the South Pole would prevent more catastrophic weather from forming, so he should work on that next, he deduced.

"Winter sprites, go throughout the northern hemisphere and spread the cold as best you can until I can get there," he told the ice creatures.

Transporting himself to the southern polar region next, he replayed the deep song, firming the ice and calming the wind and waves. The floats of ice and icebergs began to slowly rejoin, and more water froze and lifted to reform the sunken landscapes. The Earth's water level ceased its climb, and the rising oceans that threatened low-lying islands and coasts began to diminish and sink back.

"Now, to deal with those volcanoes..." Frost panted from exhaustion, nearly bent over and bracing against his knees. "How can I do that without Leaf?"

"You can't," said a too-cheerful voice at his ear.

Frost whirled around and raised his hand to smack the offender away. Then saw tiny leaves swishing in auburn hair, and moss-speckled skin. "Oh, it's you. I thought I heard an annoying insect. Turns out, I was right."

"Haha, good to know your harsh sense of humor hasn't changed." Leaf flashed him a grin. His injuries were gone, and the gash with its black veins on his shoulder was no more. He looked like his old self again. "Listen, I... I'm sorry about locking you away and beating you up and...all that. I was worse than a jerk." He scratched the back of his head and glanced down awkwardly.

Frost shrugged and looked away; they really didn't have time for this. "Yes, you were. Glad you understand. And if you've learned your lesson, I'll try not to hold a grudge. But right now, I expect you to work your butt off."

Leaf smirked in return. "Ready to cool down some lava fountains, then?" he asked, and brandished a new summer flute.

"*Heh*, I've always wanted to try icing down lava." Frost brushed his hand through his hair, flicking a spatter of snowflakes at Leaf.

Leaf made a show of dodging them as if they were diseased.

Icing down lava, however, was a messy business, as they soon discovered. The cold air and frigid water did make the lava flows slow down, but it also created billows and clouds of blinding steam. And to prevent other volcanoes from erupting involved Leaf having to carefully shift the earth beneath the pools of lava to let them drain down—a task that took great care and intense work, so as to avoid causing any earthquakes.

Frost barely registered the passing of days and nights as they both worked to restore order. After the Ring of Fire was finally calmed down, they hurried to tackle the typhoon and hurricanes, and transferred rainstorms to wash over the blazing wildfires.

Weather demons hissed and raged at them all the while, slicing their claws through the air and hissing out venomous spittle.

But with the new winter lyre and summer flute, the Season Guardians battled on and finally prevailed.

Norah waited in the Irish town, using the debit card Frost

had given her earlier to stay at a bed-and-breakfast. Two days had passed, and she watched as the weather overhead improved to a calm, steady drizzle, which locals told her was more normal for Ireland. She finally let herself start to relax.

Her phone rang. She picked it up off the windowsill where she sat waiting.

It was Tim.

"Tim, how are you? Is there enough food in the condo?"

"Yeah, there's enough. I haven't gone outside at all since you left. But the weather looked better today—no more tornado warnings, anyway."

"Good." Relief swam through her voice.

"Sis, when are you coming back? You still haven't told me what's going on, y'know. I'm your only brother, so you have to tell me everything—no more secrets!"

Norah smiled at that and picked up her coat. "Dawn. I'm catching a flight out at dawn," she told him.

Even if Frost had asked her to wait, staying in Ireland away from Tim any longer would fill her with more worry. Besides, the winter sprites hadn't exactly given her time to pack any luggage before she'd been dumped here on the other side of the ocean.

"Sweet! See you soon!" Tim hung up.

Norah pocketed the phone and shrugged on her coat. With the turn of the weather, it must mean that Frost had succeeded. He probably had his hands full straightening things out around the globe right now. She should head home; Tim needed her.

An hour and a half later found her getting out of a taxi at the nearest large airport. Some flights had been reopened due to milder skies, and two of them were headed to America— one of which was to Boston.

"Good. Things really have calmed down," she said under her breath.

She hurried with her ticket to board the large plane, stumbling down the tunnel-like boarding ramp.

When she found her seat, at the very back row against a window, she let her muscles relax and plugged in her earphones. Jazz played softly while she observed some workers outside in the cold hosing off the plane's wings.

It was her first real plane ride. Runways and lush grass passed by her small window as the plane drove around the area for a while. And then, there came a burst of speed and the sudden feel of lift off as the plane's wheels left the ground.

Norah clutched her armrests in a death grip, ear canals popping. Her stomach dropped and her head became a fuzzy nausea as the ground shrank beneath her. Clouds passed her window, and the many layers of the atmosphere became visible with all the different shapes and sizes of fluffy white condensation.

It was magical, reminding her of her flights with Frost. Although, they had never soared *this* high—she wouldn't have been able to breathe if they had.

Up here in the early morning, it felt like the plane was chasing after the fleeing remnants of night, with dawn making rosy the clouds behind her and stars clinging to the sky and blue-tinted clouds up ahead.

She finally let herself start to relax.

Norah wasn't sure when she'd dozed off, but a sudden jolting of her seat woke her up sharply. The plane itself was shaking all around her, she realized, and the passengers clung to their seats.

The intercom urged people to remain seated.

The only other person in the back row, sitting across the aisle from her, was a young hippie guy. And he was busy telling his friend seated in front of him that: "It's just a bit of bad turbulence, dude."

The shaking came in jolts and spurts. The view beyond her window was a mass of gray clouds, some of them almost charcoal black.

"Didn't they see this storm on the radar, man?" the friend panicked.

"Planes fly through storms every day. We'll be fine, just chill," the hippie replied.

The shaking returned, making Norah feel like she was in an earthquake. Suddenly, the overhead bins broke open and luggage fell out—crashing down on the passengers. Flight attendants hurried to hold onto something, unable to stand. Everywhere, people cried out, whether out of fear or from luggage hitting them, or both.

Norah tried to duck her head. Being against the window kept her farther from falling objects, but she could also see the forks of lightning that lit up the storm outside.

What a way for her first flight to turn out, she thought wryly.

One burst of light made after-images in her vision, and between blinks she could make out sparks and billows of smoke that were not a part of the storm.

The left wing's engine—it had been hit!

Thunder made a sharp, ear-splitting roar, and children's screams mixed with the chaos. The intercom turned on, once again calling for people to stay firmly buckled in their seats—as if anyone would do otherwise, stricken by terror high in the skies. Even the hippie was hunched over and clinging to his seatbelt.

"We will be turning the flight around shortly," the intercom was saying. There was no mention of the damaged engine, just that they were heading back to Ireland.

Great, that meant they were somewhere over the Atlantic Ocean—with an engine that didn't work.

She curled herself into a tense ball.

A few more minutes of turbulence passed, and Norah thought she saw the wing get struck again by lightning.

Was it just her, or did the plane seem to be tilting forward and down a bit, now?

Surely they couldn't be near land yet.

Clouds rushed upwards beyond the window, layers of white and charcoal passing above them.

They were descending. And the darkness below them was the ocean.

The plane was falling, though perhaps trying to fall with some amount of grace.

She wondered if it would even matter once they crashed into the waves and broke apart.

20

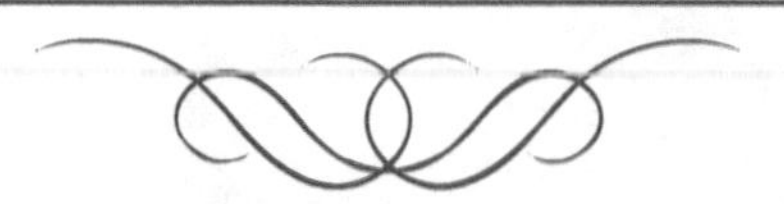

THE ICE SWORD PIERCED THROUGH the weather demon's heart.

The creature shriveled and shrank in on itself before dispersing in a wave of ashes—the final demon, now vanquished.

Frost let his ice armor melt away and the sword vanish. He panted heavily.

Leaf gave him a thumbs-up, himself bent over and sweating just as much.

"Just so you know, I'm still fuming mad at you," Frost huffed.

Leaf didn't have the energy to respond but gave a weary grunt.

A buzzing squeak at his ear made Frost suddenly jerk his head. A winter sprite hovered there, icy wings buzzing in a pattern of speech that only other sprites and insects could understand, though over the years Frost had decoded what certain sounds meant.

"What? Trouble…sinking…human?" Frost deciphered.

"Humans are drowning somewhere?" guessed Leaf.

The sprite circled him once before sailing off, northward.

Frost exhaled. "I'm taking a *long* nap once this is all over." Then he flew after the sprite.

Leaf shrugged his weary palms up in the air and followed.

The sprite hurried at a dangerous speed, ignoring its own weariness to lead Frost, and he realized this must be more serious than he thought.

Once he followed the sprite down into a dive towards the ocean's surface, he spotted a massive white shape bobbing in the unsteady waves.

Screams rent the air as people were struggling to climb out.

A European airliner—and somehow having landed on the surface of the ocean without breaking apart.

People in the water, who clung to the craft, were turning blue with hypothermia, and those still trapped inside would soon drown as the plane gradually sunk.

"Leaf, make rafts!" ordered Frost. He hoisted ten children out of the water and set them on warm wooden rafts Leaf had woven.

At their whistles, both winter and summer sprites came, helping to pull more people out of the cold. The summer sprites became like heaters, blasting warm air with their wings to melt the chill on their skin.

The humans couldn't see them but felt themselves being carried. The rafts would seem like a hallucination and all of this some nightmarish dream. They wouldn't remember what had really happened, later.

Leaf wrapped the plane in vines to hold it together and grew rafts underneath to lift it up above the waves.

Water poured out of the emergency exit doors in a whooshing rush, lightening the airliner. Frost ducked his head inside. There were two people trying feebly to reach the open doors, and now with the water flooding outward, they tumbled forward. Frost caught them and handed them back to Leaf.

It wasn't normally their job to go on rescue missions and interfere with the natural order of life and death, but the world's current mess had been their doing. If it hadn't been for their squabble, the plane might not have hit such harsh weather and gone down.

Frost continued to the back of the plane, checking seats. Water had pooled at the very back—the seats there would have been the first to drown. Thankfully, it didn't look like anybody was still—

Oh no. Water rushing out revealed a body, slumped over two seats, brown hair covering the girl's face.

Shoot… They'd been too late to save the poor girl, whoever she was.

Frost moved to free her of a tangled seat buckle, and her head slid against the seat back, some of her hair moving aside.

His fingers halted around the buckle. He stared down at her for one stricken moment before he brushed the rest of her hair back and caught her face in his hands.

It was.

It was her.

It was Norah.

Words couldn't describe the shock and the mix of horror and burning pain that suddenly filled his chest.

Norah was…

She was…

"Frost, everything okay back there?" called Leaf.

When he didn't respond, Leaf waded his way down the aisle. "Frost?"

"Dead."

Leaf stopped short of him. "Oh…were we too late to save one?"

"She's dead," Frost repeated and his voice hitched. His vision of her face in his hands blurred.

Leaf's legs sloshed through the water. "Here, let me take the girl out. Go and make sure those people are staying on the rafts."

But when Leaf edged around Frost to see the girl, what Frost had meant struck him like thunder. It wasn't just any girl—it was the only girl Frost had ever grown to care for. The girl Leaf had come to like and laugh with.

"What…what in the blazes is she doing *here*?" Leaf cried out.

Sobs suddenly racked through Frost, and he crouched, bent over, holding her hand between his palms. "Norah…I told you to wait! I told you…!"

His world felt like it was ripping in two. Once again, he was forced to endure losing someone dear to him. Even though he had resisted letting her into his heart, she'd somehow managed to sneak inside anyway. And the pain of loss was too much to bear.

He felt Leaf's hand grip his shoulder. "Frost, her soul hasn't left yet. Look."

Frost raised his head.

A translucent replica of Norah floated quietly above her body, looking both confused and anxious.

"Norah…" Frost reached up to touch her hands. Their skin met, but in an unreal way, like trying to touch water. "I'm so sorry, Norah! I'm so sorry."

He felt her palm cup his cheek. "It's okay. I won't hold a grudge forever." She smiled.

The lump in his throat tightened. "Norah, there is one way you can live again," he told her. She lowered to stand on the aisle with them, her feet floating above the floor. "It's the same way the old Guardian saved me. Take my place as Winter Guardian, now—you've been trained well enough. All you have to do is agree to take on the job."

Her hazel eyes searched his face. "I can't take your life, Frost. It would hurt too much." She glided past them and floated out of the plane.

Frost stumbled and hurried to fly after her.

Several yards above the plane wreck, he caught her liquescent shoulders and spun her to face him. "Please, Norah, don't abandon me to live alone again!" His voice choked, raw. "Think of Tim—you can't just leave him."

Her sorrowful gaze turned to the side. "But..." Her brow furrowed in misty creases. She knew he was right.

"Take my place, Norah." Frost's hands took each of hers, entwining his fingers through her misty ones. "It's my time to go. My family is waiting, and...I'll be waiting for you."

A tear shimmered down her soul's cheek, trailing to her chin. She forced a smile. "Okay. If that's what you really want, Frost."

No. What he wanted was for them *both* to be together! But there wasn't a way for that to be, and so...

"Yes, it is," he finally said.

"Then, Frost, I hereby accept—"

"Wait! Wait, wait, wait, you two crazy love doves." Leaf barreled into them, separating their hands. "Don't go leaping into a tragic storyline, just yet! There's a better solution to this mess."

"Leaf, what are you talking about?" Frost started.

But Leaf held up a silencing finger. "She doesn't have to take *your* place, when she can take my place, instead."

Puzzlement and then understanding dawned over Frost's

features. "Leaf, you… You can't mean you want to…"

"Die?" He shrugged. "Why not? I've been doing this job longer than you have, Snowflake. And while I know she trained for winter," he nudged Norah with an elbow, "I'm pretty sure she'd make a fine Summer Guardian too. Think of all the fun arguments you two could have? Except you'll probably listen to *her* more than you ever listened to *me*." He mock tilted his head, arms akimbo.

"Leaf…" Norah's features filled with a new sadness.

He gripped her right hand, giving it a squeeze—or however you do that with a liquid, misty soul. "It's all good, missy. I'm more than ready to move on to the next world!"

Her jaw worked, not knowing what to say.

"Just speak the words: you accept to be the Summer Guardian. That's all." He flashed her his brightest, warmest grin.

Her soul was starting to drift upwards, pulled by an invisible tether. Time was running out.

"I'll miss you, Leaf."

"And I you, you tough New Englander."

Her lips quirked in a laugh. She nodded to him and opened her mouth to speak the words.

"You do not have to pass away, yet."

A voice with the echo of waters spoke, and the scenery around them all shifted, until they were standing in the grand, colorful Hall of Seasons.

Frost faced the Nymph of Seasons waiting for them at the throne dais, and out the corner of his eye, he caught Norah's gaping expression of wonder and shock. "What do you mean, Lady Seasons?" he asked.

Petals fell about the translucent figure in a new, almost merry way. "A significant change has been allowed," she spoke to them. "I do not wish for any of you to feel alone, any longer. At first, I believed it was for the best that you work in solitude. But now, I see that this has caused more trouble than it has prevented," she admitted softly.

"And so, it has been granted at my request to create one more Winter Guardian and one more Summer Guardian. From now on, there will be two for each season, to better cover the world and to support one another."

Her palms spread out to Norah. "Is your wish to become that second Winter Guardian, young one?"

Norah blinked, her mouth agape as if trying to swallow a giant fruit in surprise. "Y-yes." She finally found her voice. "Yes!"

The Nymph nodded her head gracefully, and above her open palms a light flashed. There hovered a new winter lyre, decorated with frozen leaves, and it floated across to Norah.

The moment her hands took hold of the wood and icy strings, a burst of snowflakes and power whirled around her. Her physical body materialized around her soul, clothed in a deep blue dress, and feathery frost trailed up her arms and shoulders, and snowflakes glittered in her hair. Her irises, hazel, were rimmed in feathers of ice, the same as Frost's.

Norah twirled in place, her wide eyes full of wonder, and she reached to feel her new, pointed ears.

The Nymph turned to Leaf. "As punishment for your actions, the second Summer Guardian will be in charge of spring and summer. You will simply be their assistant and do as they say."

Leaf gave a meek head nod.

"For the second Summer Guardian position, who do you recommend? Who would be willing to spend the many years ahead with you?"

Frost and Norah shared a quizzical look.

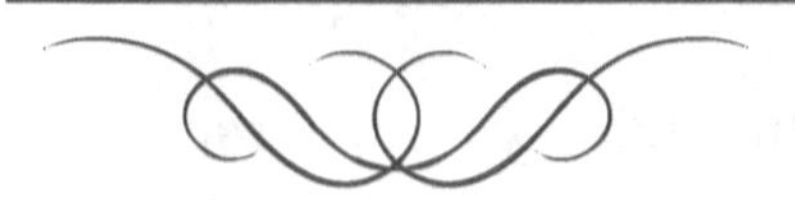

NORAH TOUCHED THE LEAF WITH her finger. Where she touched it blossomed red like vermilion drops of paint. The next leaf she imagined to be orange, and its green color brightened into sunburst orange blotches.

"Norah, hurry up! You can't spend your time being artistic with every single leaf."

She looked up at Frost, where he perched on a thick branch in the forest canopy, waving his left hand about like a paintbrush while his right hand strummed a mellow song on his winter lyre. Autumn colors rained down upon the leaves and trees all around him.

She sniffed. "But I *like* being artistic. And surely there are some humans who will appreciate my effort."

Frost's answer was a laugh.

"You dare laugh at my art?" She smirked mischievously and flew up to the branch, and he leaped off. She chased after him through the canopy, high above the forest floor, autumn blooming behind them in colorful glory where they passed.

He caught her hands and together they whirled around and around above the golden and ruby treetops.

As their spin slowed, his gaze took in every part of her, including her cute snowflake leggings and faery winter dress. He used to do this job alone, spreading the cold seasons to each hemisphere, but now there was someone to laugh with, to dream with, to experience the wonders of life with.

He drew her close and pressed his lips to hers.

She curled her arms around his neck, drawing him in, while autumn leaves and snowflakes twirled on a dancing breeze around them.

Leaf glided through Concord, the summer flute to his lips playing a song of new life. The trees along the streets and parks burst into flower, and their sweet fragrance filled the air—cherry blossoms, plums, pink magnolias, and azaleas.

He headed for the river, next, and hovered above its glittering waters.

Selk was on the bank, coaxing shrubs and weeds to sprout from the watery mud of left-over winter.

Leaf strolled leisurely up to her. "All the flowers have been sprung, as you ordered, my lady!" He gave a bow, and observed her work on the weeds closely. "You've done a marvelous job here!" He beamed proudly. "See? I knew this would be a piece of cake for you! Or rather, a piece of kelp."

She didn't catch the joke. "Yes, I do so love bringing the beauty of spring to others," she said with a toothy smile, her green hair speckled in flowers that continually bloomed.

"Strangely, I prefer warm water to cold, now. I did not think that would be possible."

He shrugged playfully. "That's the magic of becoming a Summer Guardian! And now, I finally have someone who shares my opinion when it comes to that condo's interior décor." His grin tweaked evilly.

Selk laughed, a burbling sound like a merry brook. "It is a good thing the condo is so big."

"For sure! It's become like home, hasn't it? A place to rest when the workday is done. I'm glad we all decided to keep living there." He smiled thoughtfully, and the vines in his hair shook their leaves.

Selk grinned and rose to her webbed feet. Her hand caressed his cheek. "It is a nice home."

He ran a hand through her silky, green hair. "Thank you for taking my offer—becoming my partner and all."

Her cheeks pinked. "To be with you sounded like a wonderful life."

He wrapped her in a bear hug.

But their moment was soon interrupted by a shout: "Hey! *There* you are!"

Leaf turned to see Tim come trotting down the river path toward them.

"School's out. I need a lift back home," he said.

Leaf heaved a dramatic sigh. "This is the tenth time. Have I become your personal taxi, now? I might have to start charging a fee."

Tim made his eyes large and innocent and blinked up at him pleadingly. "You wouldn't!"

Leaf winked in Selk's direction.

Selk laughed and began to summon a vortex of flower petals. "I won't charge you, little brother of Norah. I will taxi you for free."

"Hey!" Leaf mock protested.

Bob peered through the binoculars at the opposite luxury condo and its wide windows. There was even more greenery and icicles about the place, and just now a series of plates had carried themselves through the air and over to the kitchen.

"Ghosts? The ghosts are moving plates?" he muttered to himself while he watched.

One person came into view: a boy, walking alongside the plates and talking to nothing.

Behind Bob, Norah's mom grumbled around a wine bottle over at the kitchen table. "Can't you forget about your superstitions for one second and pay attention to me?"

Bob let the binoculars drift down to his chest. "Day in and day out, I keep seeing these strange things… I can't take this anymore. I can't! I want answers! I want that flat thoroughly investigated."

He grew more determined than ever. And soon as morning came, Bob dressed himself in a fine suit, to look important, and marched over to the neighboring luxury building, striding through the foyer and across to the main desk.

"May I help you, sir?" asked the well-dressed lady there.

"I want to speak to this building's manager, promptly! There's a dire situation that needs addressing."

"Ah… Well, I'll see if he's available." She called on a phone while Bob stood waiting, perching his elbow on the desk, foot tapping impatiently. "Yes, he's on his way," she told Bob shortly. "But he did ask me to make a note of what the problem is?"

"Oh, yes. So, here's the thing," he began. "Every evening when I'm in my living room, I look across and see strange things going on through the windows of one of your high-up condos."

"Strange…*things*?" she asked through an uncertain smile.

"Strange things! Icicles and frost coating the balcony and furniture, and all sorts of plants growing like a jungle about some rooms. But that's not *even* the strangest thing." He leaned close, conspiratorially. "I've seen objects move, carried through the air by invisible beings. Why, just last night a row of dinner plates up and lifted themselves! And the food on them eaten!"

"Mm-hm." The lady nodded carefully, faking a pleasant expression but for a twist of her lips.

"Weird things are happening in there, I tell you. You need to bring in a psychic! Or whatever those ghost-tracker people are called."

"And what room number are you in?" she inquired, jotting down notes.

"Uh, I'm actually in the building next door…"

"You're filing a complaint when you don't even live here?" She lifted her chin. "Are you spying on our residents, sir?"

"Huh? N-no, it's not like that—"

"What did you say your name was?" she said a little too sweetly.

"Nothing, never mind." Bob jerked his head away and pocketed his hands. He made to leave, second guessing his decision to come here.

But just then the manager arrived, and the lady pointed Bob out as the one causing a bother.

Bob hurried his footsteps. But the manager caught him at the glass doors.

"Your name and license, please?" the man asked, his large frame towering over Bob.

"Mm… Is that really necessary?"

Norah and Frost came through the door with a flurry of snowflakes and winter chill. Over at the kitchen counter to the right, both Leaf and Selk hugged their arms and shuddered.

"Couldn't make a more chilling entrance, could you?" Leaf said, pointedly eyeing the feathers of ice forming in their footsteps.

"At least you can always melt it away!" Norah gave his shoulder a pat.

The oven beeped, and Selk hurried to pull out a large casserole dish. "Look, Norah! My first attempt at human cuisine is a success!"

She proudly carried over the dish to the table, where Tim was already setting out plates and cups.

"That's a thing of beauty, right there!" Leaf nodded with pride.

Norah surveyed the extra cheesiness of the mac-and-cheese casserole. "Anything with plenty of cheese is a masterpiece to me. Nice work, Selk!"

Selk wore a pleased blush.

"Did you have a good day at school?" Norah asked Tim at the table.

"Yeah, if you don't count the stress of oncoming exams."

They all laughed at that, except for Selk, who had never experienced such things.

"Hey, Norah. I heard that guy Bob was arrested a few days back. Something to do with previous fraud and money laundering," Leaf informed.

"Really?" She and Tim shared a look. "Somehow, I'm not surprised," Norah said with a frustrated headshake. "Maybe Mom will go and get a decent job, now, and start a new life for herself, instead of relying on wealthy boyfriends."

Tim's expression showed that he wished the same, too.

Leaf opened up a bottle of high-quality sparkling grape juice, savoring its sweet aroma and sizzle. "There's no better way to celebrate the coming of spring than with grapes! Here." He filled each of their crystal glasses.

"The coming of autumn, you mean," interjected Frost.

Leaf gave a loud mock sigh, his glass in hand. "Must you make *everything* about you? Here in New England, it's spring now. We're not in the southern hemisphere. And so, to springtime we toast!"

"To springtime!" Selk raised her glass.

"I do enjoy spring more," said Tim under his breath.

Norah bumped his arm playfully. "Traitor."

They gave a toast to new life and new hope.

Norah sipped the sparkling juice and thought back over the years, of all that she and Tim had come through. Seeing bonfires still bothered her, but not nearly as much as before. Being brought back to life had given her a new perspective on many things. Plus, there was some good news that Aunt Karin was starting to regain the use of her legs. They should go visit her soon. It wasn't going to be easy keeping the whole Guardian thing a secret from her, though.

Norah sent a silent prayer of thanks, and brought her fork of pasta up to her lips.

"Things turned out all right in the end, didn't they?" Tim said from beside her.

She glanced from the pasta to him. "Yes, they did." She ruffled his hair with her free hand. "Now, less talking and more eating! Selk, this mac-and-cheese is divine."

THANK YOU

Thank you for reading! After spending many years in New England, I knew I had to write a story that featured some of my favorite places in the area (and that also described the woes of winter I've experienced, lol, with many a power outage, and the bitter chill of nights without heat—especially during the huge ice storm of 2008, when we had no electricity for two weeks).

I've always loved the different takes on Jack Frost in films and books, and so I made my own New England twist (with a dash of Irish lore) to the tale that I hope you enjoyed!

Fun fact: I took a flight out of Boston once and saw the exact scene Norah does from the plane, with the dawn chasing away the night. It was truly magical.

If you read Frost: Winter's Lonely Guardian and want to share it with other readers, please consider leaving a review on Amazon and Goodreads. This makes a huge difference for indie authors like me! Reviews help boost a book on retailer websites so that it'll be found by more readers, which in turn helps support the author.

You can be the first to learn about new releases, get bonus content, free ebooks and book sales by signing up for my newsletter at:

eerawls.com

Above all, thanks be to the Creator, who makes me able. To learn more about Him, visit:
PeaceWithGod.net/where-is-god

Reader Insider Vault

Here You'll Get Access To:

- My Curated **No-Spice Book Lists**
- Bookish **News**, *Recs & Merch*
- **Behind the Scenes** details + First Looks + *Fun Bonuses* of my books
- **Free ebooks** & more!
- My **Exclusive Newsletter** & Substack: *where you can follow my author updates & fun random finds!*

eerawls.com

Scan QR Code:

THE ALTEREDVERSE

Books in the *Alteredverse* are standalone tales that take place in our world, at different points in time, and they often feature the humanoid Altered Ones (read **Portal to Eartha** for the origin story of the Altered).

They can be read in any order. Some books take place during our time, and some far into the future. To see the full Timeline of events, and where each book fits, visit the Reader Insider Vault's Bonus Material page:

eerawls.com/reader-insiders

If you enjoyed the world of *Frost*, be sure to check out the other books in the *Alteredverse*. Also, check out the series **Draev Guardians** that takes place in the *Earthaverse*—the twin planet to our world (it can be read at any time and separately from *Alteredverse* books).

Suggested reading order:

- *Frost, Winter's Lonely Guardian*
- *Portal to Eartha*
- *Beast of the Night*
- *Madness Solver in Wonderland*

Beast of the Night

A one-armed, practical girl. A rude lord hiding a curse.
A dark secret with the town's fate hanging in the balance…

A Beauty and the Beast retelling with an
Austrian twist and a new breed of curse.

Future Japan.
A clue to a secret portal world.
The only hope for Lotus, an Altered girl with the
gift of Healing, on the run from the mafia.

You can get the ebook version FREE by
joining my newsletter!

Strayborn

Elemental Manipulation is a tricky business as Cyrus, a girl who can manipulate metal, and Aken the last Scourgeblood, are about to find out, in a world that is determined to either use them or destroy them…

See all purchase links at eerawls.com

Madness Solver in Wonderland
It's a crazy ride trying to keep the peace between both
Earth and Wonderland, solving cases, but somebody's
got to do it—and unfortunately that somebody is me.
Welcome to my nonsense life!

How You Can Help

Reviews help boost a book on retailer websites so that it'll be found by more readers, which in turn helps support the author. *If you read Frost, Winter's Lonely Guardian and want to share it with others, please consider leaving a review on Amazon and Goodreads*—this makes a huge difference for indie authors like me! It doesn't have to be much, just click on how many stars you want to rate the book, and maybe add a sentence or two on your thoughts.

8 Ways to Support an Indie Author:

See a list of all the ways you can help support my work, as well as other indie authors!
Scan the QR code:

Author

E.E. Rawls is the product of a traveling family, who even lived in Italy for 6 years. She loves exploring the unknown, whether it be in a forest, the ruins of a forgotten castle, or in the pages of a book. Her brain runs on coffee, cuddly cats, and the mysterious beauty of nature while she writes.

Visit her online at **eerawls.com** and get free access to the Reader Insider Vault:

Reader Insider Vault

Here You'll Get Access To:
- My Curated **No-Spice Book Lists**
- Bookish **News**, *Recs & Merch*
- **Behind the Scenes** details + First Looks + *Fun Bonuses* of my books
- **Free ebooks** & more!
- My **Exclusive Newsletter** & Substack: *where you can follow my author updates & fun random finds!*

eerawls.com
Scan QR Code